Eligible RECEIVER

Men of Fall #3

Eligible RECEIVER

Men of Fall #3

S.R. GREY

Eligible Receiver (Men of Fall #3)
Copyright © 2020 by S.R. Grey

ISBN-13 (print edition): 978-0-9601037-1-3

Editing: Hot Tree Editing
Proofreading: Deaton Author Services
Beta Readers: Franci N. and JoAnna E.
Cover Photographer: Wander Aguiar Photography
Model: Quin Bruce
Cover Design: Najla Qamber

Formatting: E.M. Tippetts

Other Books by
S.R. Grey

A Harbour Falls Mystery trilogy
Harbour Falls
Willow Point
Wickingham Way

Laid Bare novella series
Exposed: Laid Bare 1
Unveiled: Laid Bare 2
Spellbound: Laid Bare 3
Sacrifice: Laid Bare 4

Chapter ONE

Lonely Hearts Club
Becca

I ask myself, *Where do lonely hearts go?*

The answer is this: *They go here, Becca.*

With a quiet snort of acceptance of my lot in life, I make my way down the dimly lit center aisle of the old retro movie theatre on the outskirts of Columbus, Ohio.

With my oversized tub of buttery popcorn balanced in the crook of my elbow, I slip my black leather gloves into the pocket of my khaki trench coat. It's hanging loosely on me since I unbuttoned it after I bought my ticket out in the lobby.

Stopping, I stare at the big movie screen.

A projection of the movie poster for a classic romance flick, one from the middle of last century that is playing tonight, flickers in the low light.

I've never heard of the film, but I needed something to do.

Otherwise, I may go crazy.

Why?

Because it's freaking Valentine's Day, my least favorite holiday of the year, and I have no one to spend it with.

Par for the course, Becca.

Sighing, I glance around.

I pretty much have my choice of seats, as the theatre is mostly empty.

I guess only us lonely hearts, losers-in-love types are here to watch a sad, sappy old black-and-white movie on a day devoted to love.

The smell of popcorn wafting up to my nose distracts me, and I gingerly dig in, grabbing a healthy handful.

Hey, don't judge.

A girl needs to treat herself once in a while, especially when she's feeling this sad and alone.

That is definitely me right now.

As I eat popcorn in the middle of the aisle, like a misfit fool, I try to figure out where I'd like to sit.

There are two middle-aged ladies at the end of a row close to the front, so yeah, not there.

There's also a really old dude to my right, seated in a center spot.

No, not there either.

I glance over my shoulder to assess what's available in the back half, and that's when I spot someone in the last row, middle seat.

Hmmm…

It's a guy, for sure. Though it's hard to tell what he really looks like, especially since he's dressed in dark clothes and has a ball cap pulled a little over his brow.

Still, I can see he's young like me.

I'm twenty-five, and I'm thinking he can't be that much older.

There's an air about him too, a palpable sense of confidence, expressed in the way he's seated, leaned to one side with a kind of cocky smile on his face.

We make eye contact.

Eek, he's caught me looking back at him.

At least, I think he has.

In any case, I pretend to be deeply interested in the projector window way up high.

I'm so smooth.

Or so I think.

I guess I'm not, though, as when I venture another furtive glance at the man, it's clear he's smirking.

Whatever, dude.

I roll my eyes at him, hoping he can see.

I can't lie, though.

My interest is piqued.

I mean, come on, this dude is at a theatre on Valentine's Day, sans date, just like me.

Maybe we can start a lonely hearts club?

Sounds like a plan to me.

So rolling back my shoulders, I start toward the back row.

I may as well sit near this new potential inductee into my make-believe club.

As I close in, I'm afforded a better view of the guy.

And whoa, he is hot.

His eyes are dark in the shadows, so it's hard to tell the exact color. But the little bits of hair sticking out from under his ball cap show me the shade is chestnut-brown.

And this guy has a nice muscular build.

I'm more interested now.

My best friend, Jodi, would be so proud of me, taking charge like this.

She'd probably say, "Go for it, girl. Sit right the hell next to him. You never know what could happen."

Jodi is pretty much all about me finding a man these days. She's worried there's something wrong since I haven't gone out on a date in months.

I sigh.

There is something wrong—I've lost my *go-love* mojo.

See, I used to be the biggest romantic, like, ever. I was a hardcore serial dater, looking for love, convinced I'd find it online. I belonged to so many damn dating sites that it wasn't even funny. Some of them were downright bizarre.

One of the wackier ones was devoted to meeting your match via a blind date.

Looking back, it's probably for the best that I removed my profile from *that* particular site.

Before I did, it actually worked out for Jodi.

Not that she was on it.

No, she just took my place on a blind date one fateful night and inadvertently met a man named Caleb. He's a football player for the Columbus Comets, so score one for her.

He's the true love of her life.

Some people have all the luck.

Jodi used to talk about setting me up with one of Caleb's teammates. She still does sometimes, but I quickly change the subject.

There's no point.

Remember, I don't believe in love anymore.

Or rather, I don't believe in it for me.

And that's a truly sad state of affairs when I happen to co-own a wedding consultant business with Jodi.

When we first started, I was such a hopeless romantic.

But that was then.

And this is now.

That's why it's weird that I'm heading to the last row of the theatre, so that I can sit close to the good-looking guy in the ball cap.

I guess a part of me is finally taking Jodi's advice and saying *what the hell.*

Or maybe there's another part of me—and this is probably closer to the truth—that is freaking tired of being lonely.

It's Valentine's Day, people!

I can at least *pretend* to have a date.

Still, I proceed with caution, as it may appear weird for me to just plop down right next to the guy, especially when we're dealing with a nearly empty theatre.

I don't want to come off as a complete creeper.

That's why I stop about halfway down the row.

The guy looks up.

Ooh, I was right.

He's beyond gorgeous.

Look at those chiseled features, those delicious full lips.

I shake my head.

Get a grip, Becca.

He nods.

I nod back.

I do so coolly, though, so he doesn't think I'm back here for him.

Though I totally am—*hee hee.*

Lingering a few seats away, I say, "You don't mind if I sit in this last row with you, do you?"

He smirks knowingly—*smug ass*—and I hastily amend, "I don't mean *with you,* with you. It's just that I, uh, get vertigo if I sit too close to the screen."

"Well, this is definitely not close," he says, his voice smooth and cool.

"No, no it's not," I babble back, not smooth and cool at all.

Shrugging, he says, "I don't mind the company."

"Cool. Thanks."

I sit down, leaving two barrier seats between us.

See, I'm prudent.

After a beat, I hold out my cardboard tub of popcorn, shaking it lightly. "Hey, I'm open to sharing," I say.

That makes the man chuckle.

But then the smartass holds up a hand and retorts, "No thanks.

I'm good."

"Whatever." I pull the popcorn back, huffing. "Suit yourself."

I'm not sure how to take my, er, uh, neighbor.

He is insanely good-looking, yes, especially up close, but he's also rather cocky.

Lucky for him, I'm a sucker for arrogant pricks.

Chapter TWO

What Movie?
Lars

*T*hank Christ this chick has no idea who I am.

I was worried at first that she may have recognized me as a pro football player, and that's why she was heading back to my row.

Now I think she's just lonely.

Like me.

Why the hell else would I be at this old retro theatre on fucking Valentine's Day?

I'm not the least bit interested in the ancient movie that's playing. I just couldn't stomach the idea of sitting alone in my big ole empty house.

Not tonight.

You'd think playing football as a very skilled wide receiver for the Columbus Comets, I'd have a lot of women wanting to go out with me.

I do, but they're not the type I'm interested in.

I have no desire to waste time with annoying sports groupies who are only looking to land a professional sports player—*any* professional sports player.

They don't care who it is, or what they play.

As corny as it sounds, I want someone to want me for me.

I guess that's why this girl who is standing a few feet away from me, not knowing who I am, is so refreshing.

Nervously, she asks, "You don't mind if I sit in this last row with you, do you?"

Do I mind?

Hell, no.

I smirk at the way she's worded her query.

Hurriedly, noting my wry smile, she retorts, "I don't mean *with you*, with you. It's just that I, uh, get vertigo if I sit too close to the screen."

Sure, pretty lady.

You're not fooling me.

You may not know who I am, but it's clear you like the way I look. And that is why you came back to this last row. Don't deny it. I see it in your pretty aqua eyes.

Playing it cool, just to keep her on her toes, I say, "Well, this is definitely not close."

"No, no it's not," she stammers.

More gently, I tell her, "I don't mind the company."

I don't.

Not if it's her.

She's attractive in an understated kind of way.

I like the way her faded jeans hug her slender hips. And the swell of her breasts under the fuzzy purple sweater she has on beneath her open coat has caught my eye.

And my interest.

She's not wearing much makeup. Not that she needs any. This girl is naturally pretty. Her hair is a honey-blonde shade, and she has it pulled up in a high ponytail, making her appear fun and sporty.

I like it.

I like her.

When she sits down, she leaves two seats between us.

I almost laugh.

But I don't.

When she offers me popcorn and I decline, she yanks it and snaps, "Whatever. Suit yourself."

Crap, I didn't mean to offend her.

We sit quietly then, waiting for the movie to start.

When it doesn't—I mean, hell, not even the previews are playing yet—I try to explain. "Look, it's just that I don't like it."

"Like what?" the girl states dryly, staring straight ahead.

"Popcorn. I'm not a fan."

"Oh? Ohhh…"

She smiles over at me then, and it feels like the ice may be breaking.

Thank fuck!

With the initial awkwardness out of the way, we engage in small talk about insignificant things like what we've heard about the movie—pretty much that it's old and in black-and-white—and other mundane stuff like how nice it was today.

Great, we've resorted to chitchat about weather.

Breezily, she says, "I know. It was so mild earlier. I loved it. I'm hoping it stays this way."

"Uh, I don't think that's happening," I warn.

"No? Why not?"

I give her the bad news. "They're calling for snow this evening."

"Wait, what?" She scowls, a piece of popcorn poised halfway to her mouth.

She's so cute.

I can't help but smile.

And then I go on. "I'm afraid so. You know, it is only February, and we live in Ohio. Not exactly a tropical paradise."

"No, far from it." She laughs. "Even though I've lived here all of my life, I swear I'll never get used to the stupid snow. I actually kind of hate it."

"Huh," I counter, "I sort of like it."

"You're kidding, right?"

"No." I shake my head. "But that's probably because snow is still fairly new to me."

Appearing genuinely curious, she asks, "You're not from around here?"

"No." I twist in my seat to face her more directly. "I'm originally from Florida. I've lived in Columbus only a short while. Before that, most of the other places I lived in were warm too."

"Wow, lucky you," she says with no hint of sarcasm. "I would've stayed in one of those sunny states."

To explain to her why I didn't would blow my cover—I moved to Ohio when I was picked up by the Columbus Comets—so I just smile over at her.

There's no way I'm divulging that football brought me here, nor do I plan to share that I bought a house and am staying in town during the off-season.

No, I like that this chick has no clue who the hell I am or what I do for a living.

I plan to keep it that way.

That's why I don't mention my name, not even my first.

Even if I didn't offer up my last name—Samuels—my first name, Lars, is pretty unique. She could easily put two and two together.

Hey, she hasn't told me her name either. Though I suspect her omission is due to the fact that we've been too busy talking.

Hmm, the conversation has flowed rather nicely.

But then the lights turn all the way down to almost complete darkness and the previews begin.

We fall silent.

Though my new friend is still a couple of seats away, she leans towards me.

I do the same, shifting in her direction.

Whoa.

That's when I feel it—an electricity, a current running between us.

If I feel it, she must too, right?

I think she does, as I catch her pressing her lips together.

So I take a chance.

Patting the seat next to me, I whisper, "You should move closer."

She looks over at me, her expression indiscernible in the darkness.

Finally, she says, "Okay."

I breathe a sigh of relief that I haven't offended her.

"Cool."

Once she sits down in the seat next to me, she sets her popcorn down on the floor.

When she leans back, her arm brushes mine.

Shit, that current of electricity that's been humming soars off the charts.

I take a deep breath.

She smells sweet, like honeysuckles or something. I don't know. All I do know is that I want to drink her in.

Casually, I drape an arm around the back of her seat.

She scoots closer, her right knee touching my left.

I don't pull away, and neither does she.

Things are sizzling now.

When I blow out a stuttered breath, she glances over at me.

Even in the darkness, I can see that her eyes are definitely fucking aqua.

"Beautiful," I murmur.

Suddenly, and surprising the shit out of me, this chick I've just met fucking leans in and presses her lips to mine.

Jesus, they're soft.

I'm stunned at first and don't really respond.

I guess she takes that the wrong way, as she jerks back, shrinking down into her seat.

"Shit, I'm sorry," she mutters. "I don't know what came over me."

After turning my ball cap around so that the bill's in the back, I place my hand on her arm.

"It's okay," I whisper. "You just caught me off guard. But now that I've caught up"—I close the gap between us—"I think we need to revisit where we just left off."

"You do?"

I touch my lips to hers, brushing over them softly.

"Yes, I definitely do," I murmur.

"Okay."

I kiss her gently at first, just some little nips and soft pecks. But when she opens her mouth and our tongues touch, I forget that we're in a theatre.

All I know is honeysuckles and soft woman.

I can't stop.

I lift the hem of her sweater an inch, testing.

She groans, and I kiss her harder, moving my hand up her taut tummy, seeking out the swell of her breasts.

Through the silky material of her bra, I ply at one taut nipple.

She gasps into my mouth and places her hand on my jean-clad thigh.

Yes!

Letting out a low growl, I grab hold of her ponytail and tug.

She must like that, as she makes the sweetest little sound of assent.

She then slides her hand farther up my leg.

Up, up, up she goes.

Yeah, I'm hard as fuck now.

Going for it, she settles her hand right fucking *there*, on my cock.

Pulling back, I grind out, "Do you want to get out of here?"

She doesn't say a thing.

She just blinks at me.

Okay, this is turning sideways.

Chapter THREE

A Woman Left Lonely
Becca

*W*hat in the hell am I doing?

I'm freaking making out with a complete stranger.

A hot stranger, yes, but still a man I know nothing about.

Suddenly, all my common sense returns with a vengeance.

This guy could be a serial killer for all I know!

Or he could be some kind of a psycho in general.

Yet here I am kissing him.

Letting him feel me up.

Putting my hand on his freaking cock, for God's sake!

It felt huge, by the way.

No, stop. This is nuts.

I am nuts.

I've truly lost my mind.

I don't even know this dude's name.

And now is not the time to find out.

He wants to "get out of here."

I know what that means.

The thing that scares me is I *want* to get out of here with him.

I want to go have mindless, meaningless sex with this hot stranger.

I bet he's great in bed.

Despite all my yearning, I can't do it.

I just can't.

I'm a chicken.

Blinking at him, I jump up and stammer, "I, uh… I-I have to go."

Looking confused as all get out, stranger-man-who-could-be-a-serial-killer says, "Wait, what? Why? What's wrong? What just happened here?"

Waving my hand in the air like the lunatic he must think I am, I snap, "This, us. We are what's wrong. Can't you see that?"

"Er, um… No."

I shake my head. "Seriously, dude, I don't even know you."

Chuckling, he murmurs, "Seems like we were getting to know each other just fine."

He's back to being a smug ass, and that just pisses me off even more.

"I am so out of here," I grind out.

Spinning around, I storm off.

Thank God the exit is close.

It's especially good, seeing as that old guy in the center aisle has just noticed the commotion in the back and is turning around, shushing us.

"You can go to hell too!" I yell over my shoulder at him.

Why I just damned the old man to Hades, I don't know.

I guess I'm just frustrated.

Rushing out into the lobby, I pass through the theatre doors, and race to my car.

Thank God I found a spot right out in front.

It's snowing, just like jerk-o said it would, but it's fairly light.

I'm still so mad that it takes me a minute or two to notice it's gotten much colder.

That's kind of good.

I need to cool down.

As much as I hate snow, I'm glad it's falling. It creates a thin coating on my windshield, like a protective cover. No one can see me inside, giving me time to get ahold of myself.

I need the reprieve.

I can't drive, not yet.

I'm too worked up… in more ways than one.

Damn hot stranger!

In addition to finding myself sexually frustrated, I'm mad I did something so reckless.

What's even crazier is I'm pissed I didn't take it further.

Talk about contradictions!

"You just don't know what you want, do you?" I whisper as I take in my reflection in the rearview mirror.

It seems that I don't, not anymore.

For so long I wanted a real relationship, a romance for the ages. Despite a search for exactly that, one that extended far and wide thanks to all those dating sites, I never met anyone worthwhile.

"And now you've stooped to making out with strange men in old movie theatres." I scoff. "How the mighty have fallen. Just look at you, Becca Nadeau. What's up with you lately?"

I'm a wreck, that's what's up with me.

My lips are swollen, and loose strands of hair, having escaped from my once-neat ponytail, are sticking out everywhere.

I'm also flushed, making me look like a woman who just had a good romp in the hay with a hot-as-sin man.

Too bad that couldn't be further from the truth.

No.

Instead, I'm a woman left sexually frustrated.

A woman left feeling foolish.

And a woman left lonely.

Chapter FOUR

Take That, Cupid

Lars

I have no idea what just went down.

All I know is for a few short minutes—too short, really—I was sucking face with a sexy woman.

But now I'm sitting alone in the last row of a theatre with a goddamn hard-on, like some kind of a perv.

"Great," I murmur, adjusting myself discreetly. "Nothing like leaving me high and dry, Crazy Girl."

Of course the crazy girl is gone, the only thing lingering, letting me to know for sure she was really here, is the faint scent of honeysuckles.

I breathe in, and my erection jumps back to life.

Just wonderful.

"Fucking honeysuckles," I grind out. "I guess this means any time I smell the damn things, I'll get hard."

I have to laugh.

This should make for an interesting spring.

I sure as hell hope there aren't any honeysuckles near the practice field at the Comets' training facility. If there are, my teammates are going to wonder what's up with me. I mean, shit, no one enjoys scrimmages and running routes *that* much.

Ah, but I needn't worry.

Official practices don't start until May. I've been working out with my best friend and teammate, Caleb Fortier, but on a casual basis, as it is only February.

So, yeah, I should be good by spring.

Crazy Honeysuckle Girl will be a distant memory by mini-camp.

I chuckle to myself.

I am so going to have to tell Caleb about this bizarre night.

He'll get a kick out of it.

With a sigh, I sit back and try to watch the movie.

It's impossible, though.

It's difficult to get into something you've missed the beginning of.

Since I have no idea what's going on, I decide to just leave.

Once I'm outside, on the snow-covered sidewalk, I catch a glimpse of a car speeding away. Every instinct tells me it's the crazy honeysuckle girl, running even farther from me.

It has to be her.

I smell her honeysuckle scent.

Of course, my dick twitches in response.

Traitorous bastard.

Shaking my head, I mutter, "I need to get out of here."

Valentine's Day is beyond ruined now.

The only positive is I did get to make out with a hot—albeit crazy—chick.

Take that, Cupid!

Chapter FIVE

Consolation Prize

Becca

The next day, at our wedding consultant shop, which is really just a small storefront in a strip mall on the west side of Columbus, poor Jodi can't figure out why I'm so down.

"Is it because yesterday was Valentine's Day?" she asks, peering over at me from her desk with big, sad whiskey-colored eyes.

"No." I shake my head, my blonde ponytail swinging. "Was it Valentine's Day? Huh, I didn't even notice."

I am trying to play this off, but Jodi's not buying my clueless act. She knows me too well. We've been friends since junior high, so not much gets by her when it comes to me.

Closing her laptop lid, she states somberly, "I think we need to talk about this, Becca."

Continuing to act clueless, I ask, "Talk about what?"

"Stop it." She holds up her hand. "We need to address why you've become so anti-love lately. I mean, it makes no sense. You used to be the biggest romantic I knew. I loved that about you too." Pausing for a thoughtful beat, she goes on. "But here we are, you telling me that you didn't even freaking notice it was Valentine's Day!" She throws her hands up in the air, exasperated. "That's like Santa Claus forgetting Christmas."

"Please." I laugh. "That's a bit overly dramatic, don't you think?"

"I don't think so, Becca. Something is up. Something's been up for a while. I don't believe for a minute that you forgot Valentine's Day. In fact, I think something happened last night."

Ha, did it ever.

I made out with a possible serial killer.

How am I supposed to tell my best friend that?

Then again, if I can't share my misdeeds with her, who can I share with?

Slowly, I blow out a breath. "Okay, okay. Something did happen," I admit, pushing my chair out from under my desk so I can lean back and peer up at the ceiling. "I actually have a lot to confess."

"Go on," Jodi prompts.

I glance over at her sheepishly. "I did know it was stupid Valentine's Day, all right? But I'd like to forget that it was. In fact, I'd like to erase the whole damn night."

Frowning, Jodi asks, "Why?"

"Because I made a damn fool of myself, that's why."

"Becca, tell me what happened. I bet it wasn't that bad."

I snort. "Trust me, it was."

I place my head in my hands and let out a little cry of anguish, and Jodi rolls her chair over to me.

Softly, she says, "Talk to me, okay? I can help."

Lifting my head and peering at her dubiously, I roll my eyes. "I don't know about that."

"Try me, okay? You know we always talk these things out, and it usually ends up with both of us feeling better."

She's right, so I close my eyes and begin my tawdry tale.

"So," I sigh. "I went to some old movie last night. Not that I even watched a single minute of it."

"And why is that, Becca?"

I open my eyes. "I, uh, kind of met a guy."

Jodi, misunderstanding, gets all excited. Dropping her arm from around my shoulders, she claps her hands. "Oh my God, this is so great. Why were you afraid to tell me this? Is he cute? Is he nice? Are you going to see each other again? If so, when?"

I hold up my hand. "Whoa, wait, slow down."

"Why? Isn't this what those dating sites were all about? You always wanted to meet someone special, right?"

Exasperated, I blurt out, "Jodi, the only thing special about this guy is that he may be a serial killer!"

"Huh?"

That shuts her up, but it gets me going.

"I freaking kissed him," I cry out. "No, wait, we totally made out. I made out with a guy whose name I didn't even take the time to find out. I actually don't know *anything* about him, Jodi. Only that he is insanely hot and an amazing kisser."

Nodding thoughtfully, she says, "Well, there is that."

I smack her arm. "Stop it. Didn't you hear the part about him maybe being a serial killer?"

Rolling her eyes, Jodi says, "Of course I heard. But I'm sure he's not one. Not to mention, he must've really gotten to you for you to be so, uh, animated about the whole thing."

"Gotten to me or not, it doesn't matter."

Leveling me with a no-nonsense, we're-getting-to-the-bottom-of-this gaze, Jodi says, "What's really going on, Becca?"

I let out a groan. "I'm pathetic, that's what's going on. When things got real with me and this hot guy, I ran out like a baby. I'm sure he thinks I'm crazy. The only bright spot in this whole shit show is that I'll never have to see him ever again. Never, never for the rest of my life! Thank God. That's why I told you I wish I could erase the whole damn night. In my head, I already have." I amend, "Well, I'm trying to. Those kisses, though…"

Softly, Jodi says, "I actually think I have a great way for you to erase the whole memory of him."

"I'm intrigued." I cock my head. "What do you propose?"

Excitedly, Jodi replies, "Let's finally set you up with Caleb's best friend, Lars. We've talked about it for so long. Let's make it happen."

"Oh, I don't know, Jodi."

"Come on, Becca. There was a time you once asked me if Caleb knew anyone single and ready to mingle. You remember that, right?"

"I do," I confirm. "But that was back when I believed in love."

Jodi touches my arm. "You can believe in it again, sweetie. You're going to meet your 'one.' I just know it. In the meantime, let's set up this double date. Maybe you'll like Lars. If nothing else, it'll cheer you up and get your mind off the serial killer."

"Ha ha, smartass." I shoot her the bird.

Reaching out and lowering my hand, she says, "Hey, seriously, this could be a good thing. Caleb tells me all the time that Lars is a fun guy. Do you want to see a picture of him? He's really hot."

I think about it, but ultimately I decide if I'm going to do this I'm playing it my way. And my way is how I used to do things when I belonged to the blind date site.

Yep, I'm going in blind.

I only need to know the guy's name.

That's enough.

I don't care, anyway.

I'm not expecting a love match or anything with this Lars dude.

I'm just going out to get Jodi off of my back. Lars, schmars.

I can't tell my best friend, but, despite all my bluster to the contrary, the only man I'll be thinking about for the foreseeable future is the hot guy at the theatre… and how I totally screwed up a chance to have possibly the best night of my life.

I Kind of Like Crazy

Lars

A few days after the theatre incident, I meet up with Caleb at the team gym to work out.

We have the place to ourselves since it's the off-season.

That means we have the freedom to talk openly.

Good thing too, as I'm practically bursting at the seams to get off my chest what happened with the crazy chick at the movie theatre.

I tell Caleb about that night right away, leaving out not a single detail.

Once I'm done, he says, "Wow. That is one crazy story."

"Tell me about it," I chuff.

Wiping sweat from his brow, having just finished a series of hard reps, he asks, "Did you at least get her number?"

"Uh, no." I shake my head. "I actually didn't even catch her name."

"Man, that sucks," Caleb replies.

"Right?" I pick up a barbell and start a set of reps, focusing on my biceps. "I should've followed her out when she left. I could've gotten her name and number, maybe even asked her out on a date. It's not like I was watching the movie by that point."

I stop lifting long enough to shoot a meaningful glance over at Caleb.

He laughs. "Sounds like you're still interested in her."

I think it over and conclude, "Yeah, I am. I mean, hell, she's pretty and she definitely intrigued me. I'd see her again in a heartbeat."

Caleb scoffs. "Yeah, but I thought you said she was a little crazy?"

"She was." I nod. "But I think I kind of like crazy."

Caleb shakes his head. "Man, you must."

Smartass.

I'm quick to remind him, "Hey, you and Jodi have had your moments."

"That's true." Sitting down on the end of a weight bench, he says, "Speaking of Jodi, she brought up that fixing-you-up-with-someone idea again. Are you open to it? It could be good for you to meet a new woman. Maybe even get your mind off the crazy theatre chick."

I shrug. "Yeah, sure, I'm up for it. I'm assuming you're talking about that double date plan with her friend Becca, the one that never happened?"

"That would be the one. So what do you think?"

I scrub my hand down my face. "Ah, hell, I don't know. What does this Becca even look like? No one's ever shown me a picture."

"That's because there's no need," Caleb says, smirking. "She's pretty, man, trust me. But here, if you insist…" He reaches for his phone that is on an unused weight bench. "I can show you a photo of her. I think I have one where she's with Jodi."

My instincts tell me to take a look.

But then I change my mind.

I don't want to break it to Caleb, but it doesn't matter what this Becca looks like. I don't expect this double date to amount to anything. I'm just going out on it to put an end to this "setting me up with Jodi's friend" nonsense once and for all.

Waving my hand at the proffered phone, I say, "Nah, Caleb, I'm good. I don't need to see a photo. I think I'd rather it be a surprise, anyway. I trust you."

"You should," Caleb says as he sets his phone back down on the weight bench. "You'll be more than pleased with the way Becca looks. Plus, the girl is cool as shit. She's laid-back and always up for fun. Kind of like you. I'm telling you, Lars, you're going to like her."

Despite all his hopeful bluster, I'm doubtful.

Blind double dates are usually a recipe for disaster, right?

Even though that's my belief and no one's ever going to change my mind, I tell Caleb, "Yeah, I'm sure you're right. I'll probably think she's okay."

"She's more than 'okay,'" he insists.

"Dude, really, whatever."

Caleb quits singing this Becca girl's praises, but does go on to inform me he and Jodi will figure out the double date logistics.

"I'll get back to you once we have a solid plan," he says.

"Cool." I nod distractedly. "Whatever you guys come up with is fine with me."

We drop the subject and place our full focus back into lifting.

An hour or so later, after we wrap up, we grab a light lunch.

And then I return home.

I'm not expecting the double date to be put into motion anytime soon, as it's been delayed for-fucking-ever.

But then Caleb calls around eight.

"Dude, it's so on," he tells me. "Becca's up for meeting you, and she's free tomorrow night. Jodi and I have nothing planned either, so it's all up to you, my man. How's your schedule looking?"

I bark out a laugh. "Are you kidding me? The only thing on my planner is another boring night spent in."

"Not tomorrow night," Caleb replies.

Suddenly feeling a little excited at the prospect of doing something social, I reply, "Sounds good. So what are we doing?"

"Jodi and I are thinking maybe just a simple dinner out. That way you and Becca can have a chance to talk and get to know one another."

"Jesus." I swipe at my brow, my enthusiasm dampening. "Talk about pressure."

"No, no. No pressure at all, my friend. Jodi and I don't want it to feel like that for you or Becca. In fact, let's just meet at the restaurant, okay? We'll have Becca do the same."

"That works for me," I reply, feeling relieved.

"Eight o'clock good for you?"

"Yeah, sure, I'll be there at eight."

Caleb gives me the name and address of the restaurant, and then says, "Great. Remember, if it all goes to hell, which it totally will not, at least you'll have a getaway car."

"Cool," I deadpan. "It's reassuring to know I can make an escape if need be."

I'm already thinking of excuses to leave early, even as Caleb says, "I told you to trust me on this, Lars. You're not going to want to leave early."

Man, I don't know.

I hope he's right.

But I doubt it.

What's the chance this double date will really work out?

I'm guessing slim to none.

Chapter
SEVEN

Wait, I Know You
Becca

*T*he double date is set.

Oh, crap.

I'm nervous.

I'm happy, though, that I'll have my own car.

If I need to escape, I can.

Despite my trepidation, I'm a little curious as to what this Lars guy will be like.

Is he really as good-looking as Jodi keeps saying he is?

Is he a decent guy?

Is he funny?

I don't know.

I'm not expecting much.

If this teammate of Caleb's is so hot and nice, why is he still on the market?

"On top of that, how could he ever hope to compete with my mystery theatre guy?" I ask my reflection as I gloss my lips in a pale shade of pink.

Eek, I'm almost ready to leave the house.

I don't want to go.

I'm scared.

But I'm in it now.

I guess that's why I decided to go all out for this double date.

I only wish it were with the theatre guy.

I bet he'd appreciate my black suede thigh-high boots and slinky velvet minidress, also in black.

I'm wearing more makeup than usual, having lined my eyes in dark kohl and applied a couple of thick coats of ebony mascara. I even curled my long blonde hair so I can wear it down and at max volume.

I guess a part of me is hoping Lars is as handsome as Jodi says he is.

The little bit of me that still believes in romance is springing to life.

I can't help but hope this goes relatively well.

"Maybe Lars is your one," I whisper to my reflection. But just as quickly, I counter, "Yeah, right. Dream on, Becca. What are you thinking?"

Before I head out to the restaurant, I think about looking up Lars online, just to have a preview of what I'm in for.

But then I remind myself that it doesn't matter. Mystery Theatre Guy is the only man on my mind, even though I will never see him again.

That doesn't mean he hasn't starred in many of my fantasies lately. *Ooh, has he ever.*

With a resigned sigh, I grab my coat and keys and head out to the car.

In a matter of minutes—too soon, really—I'm turning into the parking lot of the trendy Italian restaurant where the double date is set to occur.

I'm happy to see it doesn't appear to be too busy.

Good.

The last thing I need is an audience.

I'm already nervous enough.

Ugh.

When I spot Caleb and Jodi's car, I nab the space next to it.

It's a huge relief knowing they're already here, especially since I have no idea what Lars drives or, of course, what he looks like.

My heart is beating like crazy, so I stall for time, spending a few minutes checking my reflection in the rearview mirror and making sure I look all right.

Despite my I-got-it-together attire, I look nervous.

Unfortunately, I have the kind of face that betrays my every emotion.

And tonight is no exception.

Great, this Lars guy is going to have the honor of meeting insecure, antsy Becca.

"Bet that'll really turn him on," I murmur sarcastically as I finally get out of my car and start into the restaurant.

"Here goes nothing," I whisper once I reach the entrance.

When I walk inside, I'm beyond relieved to find Jodi is waiting for me next to the hostess station.

"You are a true lifesaver," I breathe out. "And you're definitely the best friend ever."

Placing a supportive hand on my forearm, she says, "I wasn't about to make you walk to our table all by yourself."

I sort of panic then. "Eek, does that mean Lars is here?"

"Yes," Jodi confirms. "But don't worry. You look amazing, and I'm sure you two are going to hit it off beautifully."

"You look good too," I tell her, nodding to her black slacks and snow white sweater. "All sleek and put together."

"Thanks."

To stall for more time, I inquire, "Are the guys dressed up too?"

"Yeah." She nods. "They have on suits."

"Huh. Good thing I didn't opt for my usual tomboy-casual attire."

"Yeah, good call." Jodi says, urging me along. She knows I'm rambling. "Now come on. Let's introduce you to Lars. Just be you. This is simply a nice dinner amongst friends."

"If you say so," I murmur as I let her tug me along.

We head into the seating area and over to what I assume is our table. The only thing I can see of Lars is the back of his head.

Hmm, dark hair looking all sexy-messy.

"So far, so good," I murmur.

"See, I told you," Jodi whispers.

"His shoulders look good in that suit too. They're nice and wide." She laughs. "Yeah, kind of like a football player, huh?"

"Ha ha. You're such a smartass."

I know what Jodi's doing, though.

She's trying to loosen me up.

It's working too.

I feel better, more relaxed.

This is going to go well.

I just know it.

I'm pleased already that Jodi wasn't lying.

Lars is not a mutant.

Still, I need to see his face to be sure.

Just as we reach the table, Lars turns to me.

What?

Huh?

I blurt out, "Wait, I know you."

"You do?" I hear Caleb ask.

Jodi is standing next to me, peering at me with her mouth open. It's not often she's at a loss for words, but she sure is now. As is my mystery theatre man, aka possible serial killer, aka Lars.

Okay, maybe it's safe to say he's not a serial killer. I think Jodi and Caleb would be aware of that. But he *is* the hot guy I made out with the other night.

And, worst of all, he's the guy I made a fool of myself in front of.

"Fuck," I murmur.

Lars finds his voice and says, "Shit, it's you."

Suddenly defensive and ready to run, I snap, "In the flesh."

Jodi jumps in, utterly confused still. "You guys, uh, know each other? How's that possible?"

I turn to her and say, "Yeah, we know each other. We kind of met at a movie theatre the other night."

Silence descends as realization dawns on her face. "Ohhh…"

"Exactly."

I look at Lars. He's making eye contact with Caleb, and both of them are smiling knowingly. It's clear he's told his friend about our little impromptu kissing session.

Great, just great.

I feel foolish.

I feel dumb.

Why didn't I ask to see a picture of this guy?

Why didn't I look him up?

Noooo, I wanted to do it my stupid way.

Oh, well.

It's too late now.

I catch Caleb murmuring something to Lars just as Jodi is saying that we should just sit down and hash this thing out.

"No way," I snap.

And then I do what I do best—I run.

Chapter EIGHT

The Biggest Catch of My Life
Lars

*H*ell no, not again. This is so not happening a second time.

When the hot chick from the theatre takes off, I jump up from my seat and follow her.

What's the freaking chance my pseudo-hookup would turn out to be Jodi's friend?

Pretty crazy, huh?

So her name is Becca.

I like it.

I like her.

That's why she's not getting away this time.

I catch balls for a living, for Christ's sake.

I sure as hell should be able to catch her.

Of course, the balls are being thrown *to* me on the field.

This Becca chick is going the other way.

Eh, it doesn't matter.

I'm confident I'll get her.

Why do I have the feeling this could be the biggest catch of my life?

"Maybe because it could be," I murmur, racing to the restaurant exit in pursuit.

Once I'm out in the parking lot, I catch sight of Becca hurrying to her car.

This chick sure is fast.

Good thing I'm faster.

Just as she reaches the driver's side door and is about to open it, I catch up to her.

Phew!

Placing my hand on her arm, I ask, "Can you hold up a second, Becca? That is your name, right?"

Shaking me off, she spins around. "Why should I stop?" she snaps. "So you can make fun of me?"

Frowning, I ask, "Why would I do that?"

Wrapping her arms around herself protectively, she says, "Maybe because I've made a fool of myself with you not once but twice."

I'm even more boggled now, prompting me to say, "How do you see it that way?"

Uncrossing her arms, she holds up her hand and ticks off, "Hmmm, let me see… One, I looked stupid at the theatre when I practically attacked you and then ran off. And two, I just took off again like a scared little rabbit in front of an entire restaurant."

"It wasn't that full in there," I say.

"Just shut up, okay?"

Smiling, I say softly, "I kind of liked one of those things you ticked off."

"Huh?" Leaning back on the door, she peers up at me questioningly.

"I'm talking about the you-attacking-me. Not so much the running off." Narrowing my eyes, I add, "Though running does seem to be a pattern with you."

"Very funny, Lars." She huffs. "That is *your* name, right?"

Ah, so she's mocking me.

That's okay.

It's better than her running.

Chuckling, I reply, "Yes, Lars is my name, *Becca*."

Sniffing haughtily, she retorts, "Like you couldn't have mentioned that at the theatre?"

"I didn't see *you* offering up your name that night."

She waves her hand. "Okay, good point. But that was only because it slipped my mind."

I smirk. "I wonder why."

Becca shrugs like she doesn't know it was because we were too busy sucking face to exchange vital stats like our names.

Although, in all fairness, I did hold mine back intentionally.

She's obviously trying so hard to stay angry with me, but I detect the hint of a smile playing on her full lips.

Ahh, that's better.

I remember that night too, and kissing those lips was sublime.

Crossing my arms, I ask, "What are you afraid of, anyway? Why *do* you keep running from me?"

"I don't know," she admits softly.

"Ah, but I think you do. So tell me."

As her pretty aqua eyes meet mine, she says, "I run because I'm afraid of you."

Chapter NINE

You and How You Make Me Feel
Becca

Lars asks me what I'm afraid of, so I tell him the truth. "I run because I'm afraid of you."

Uncrossing his arms and pointing to his broad chest, which looks really good in the white dress shirt he has on underneath his dark suit jacket, he says, "You're afraid of *me*? That can't be right."

"It is," I reply, sighing. "Look, I'm being brutally honest here. I'm afraid of you and, well, how you make me feel."

"Ahh…" He gets it and asks softly, "Is that really a bad thing, Becca?"

"It is when a person has given up on feeling this way."

With compassion in his beautiful eyes, Lars asks if I'd be more comfortable talking in my car or in his.

There are currently no people in the restaurant parking lot, but it is a little strange to be standing around in the dark, under the glow of artificial lighting, having an important conversation.

Nodding, I say, "Okay. We can talk in my car."

I unlock the doors of my sedan, and once Lars and I are seated inside, I send a quick text to Jodi.

I want to let her know I'm okay and that I'm actually talking with Lars out in the parking lot in my car.

I explain this, and she texts back a winking smiling emoji and **Guess we should order dinner without you, huh?**

I reply, **Yes, I think so.**

I share our exchange with Lars so he knows what's going on.

"You don't mind skipping dinner, do you?" I ask him.

Raking his fingers through his dark hair in a totally sexy way, he tells me, "If it means I get to spend time with you like this alone, then no, I don't mind at all."

He's so damn easygoing.

And full of flattery.

Oh, and he's hot too.

I sigh.

Lars is everything I've been searching for. He even followed me out of the restaurant, after me running away from him *again*.

Still, I'm wary.

I don't want to end up with a broken heart.

I remind myself that Lars is a good-looking football player. He could have anyone he wants.

Why would he want boring ole me?

I just kind of sit still, not responding in any way.

My hesitancy doesn't scare him, though.

He actually goes on to say, "Maybe I can change your mind on the 'giving up on feeling this way' stuff."

"I highly doubt that." I scoff. "Sorry, but my mind's made up."

Lars lowers his voice to a sexy whisper. "Come on, Becca. Let me at least try to change your mind. Go out with me, but not on a double date. It should just be you and me. What do you say? Will you give me a chance?"

I want so badly to say, "Yes, yes, yes," but my heart won't let me.

Shaking my head, I mumble, "I just don't think it's a good idea."

Lars blows out a breath. "You know what I think?"

"What?"

"I think you're afraid of letting go, of losing control. The incident in the theatre showed me that. That's why you ran that night. Things got too real. And that's why you ran again tonight."

Bristling at the truth of his observations, I snap, "How can you say those things? You don't even know me."

Lars thinks that over, nodding contemplatively. "That's true, Becca, if you mean not knowing you in the traditional sense. But I think I can read people rather well. Maybe I know you more than you realize. Like"—he points over at me—"maybe I sense what's really in your heart. *That's* why you should give me a chance. Or better yet, give us a chance."

Rolling my eyes, I say, "Hate to break it to you, but there is no 'us.'"

"No, but there could be."

Wow, this man is persistent.

Nonetheless, I reply with a solid, "I don't think so."

Lars chuckles. "You sure are stubborn, aren't you? Funny, Caleb didn't mention that."

Curious, I ask, "What exactly did he say about me?"

"He said you were pretty."

Lars's voice is so smooth and sexy, and he just said I was pretty.

Gah!

Well, he's really just parroting what Caleb said.

But still.

Quietly, and still in that hot-as-hell voice, he adds, "He was right about that, by the way."

Oh my God, kill me now.

My resistance is waning, so I murmur a halfhearted, "Stop."

I must be blushing like crazy.

My cheeks are burning.

They grow even warmer when Lars says, "He also said you were always up for fun and you're laid-back. I think I saw more of that at the theatre, though."

Waving my hand, I reply, "Okay, enough."

Lars shrugs. "Hey, you asked me what Caleb said."

"Yeah, I did. But let's get back to me being stubborn."

Confused, he asks, "Huh?"

I can't tell him I have to change the subject. It's far safer to talk about my shortcomings than listen to him compliment me.

But since he's seems truly boggled, I clarify, "What I mean is that I am stubborn. You were right. So have you given up yet?"

Looking over at me intently, Lars raises one dark brow. "Do you want me to give up, Becca? If you really, truly do, I will leave you alone." He places his hand on the passenger side door handle, like he's about to get out of the car. "Just give me the word and I'll leave, no questions asked."

I blow out a breath as I think it over.

Do I really want him gone?

He is kind of wearing me down.

And it's not like I *never* want to see him again.

Not to mention, I have been thinking about him a lot lately, probably to an unhealthy extent.

Yeah, this gorgeous man has starred in far too many of my fantasies since the night at the theatre.

Clearly, he is the one I want.

So should I give him a chance and go out with him?

I want to deep down inside.

But there must be a condition, one that'll protect my heart.

Softly, I say to Lars, "I don't think I want you to give up."

Looking like he's just won this round, he murmurs, "That's what I thought."

But it's me who delivers the knockout punch when I retort, "I will go out with you, yes. But only as a friend."

Chapter
TEN

Friend-Zoned
Lars

"Wait, what?"

Becca says, "You heard me."

Holy hell, I sure did.

I've just been friend-zoned.

And here I thought I had her ready to capitulate.

Good thing I like her enough that I'll take what I can get.

So friend-zoned it is… for now.

Yeah, right.

We'll see how long that lasts once I woo her.

I'm not about to show my hand, though, so I simply agree. "Sure, okay. I can live with us being friends only."

Becca doesn't look like she believes me.

Wise girl.

Sounding skeptical, she asks, "Really, Lars? Can you really just be my friend?"

I roll my eyes. "Yes, Becca, I really can."

"You sure are feisty," she remarks.

"Ha! You don't know the half of it. I'll show you feisty, woman."

I'm about to lean over and kiss the ever-loving hell out of her—fuck this friends crap already—but she holds up her hand.

"Ah, ah, ah, hold up there, bud. You do realize 'friends only' means there will be no repeats of the night at the movie theatre?"

I grumble, "Right, right. Okay, I get it. No kissing."

"And no groping," she adds.

"No groping, either. I got that too."

She sounds unsure when she whispers, "And definitely, *definitely* no sex."

Eyeing her suspiciously, I ask, "Are these rules for me, or are they actually for you?"

"Very funny, jackass." She pushes my shoulder, but of course she can't budge me. "For your information, they're for both of us."

I hold up my hands. "All right, okay, I give up. We'll play it your way."

"Good. Now that we have that established, when should we go out?"

I crack a smile. "Eager, aren't we, *friend*?"

Shaking her head, her soft blonde curls bouncing, she tells me, "You are so arrogant. You know this, right? I mean, you have to. It's not just tonight. You were like this at the theatre too."

"Whatever." I snort. "Arrogant, my ass. I prefer to call it confidence."

"See what I mean?" She throws up her hands. "Good thing we're going to be just friends."

"Yeah"—I roll my eyes—"good thing."

It totally is not, but like I told her, I can play her game. What she doesn't realize is that I plan to win in the end, meaning she will be mine. I am eventually going to have her under me, screaming out my name in pleasure.

Becca, breaking me from my dirty thoughts, asks, "Do you want to go out as friends or not?"

"I want to," I confirm. "I told you as much. So yeah, let's make a plan."

"Okay, when should we go out?"

Again, her eagerness amuses me.

Maybe that does make me sound cocky, but who cares?

I'm all about winning.

And I plan to win her.

I mean, look at her in that slinky black dress and thigh-high boots. Becca is sexy and beautiful.

Wait, that gives me an idea…

I tell her as much, and she says, "What kind of an idea?"

"I think we should go out on our first date—as friends, of course—right now."

Her brows shoot up. "Go out now?"

"Yeah, why not? We still need to eat dinner, right?"

Blinking over at me and looking cute as hell, she says, "Should we go back into the restaurant, then?"

I shake my head. "Nah, Caleb and Jodi have probably already ordered their food. They may even be eating." Grinning over at her mischievously, I add, "What do you say we ditch them and go out and do our own thing?"

I can tell she likes the idea. Becca may be a runner, but Caleb was right when he said she's up for fun.

This girl is definitely coming out of her shell.

I like that.

It means we can be real with each other.

Becca agrees on starting our first "friends" date right away, and asks enthusiastically. "Do you want to follow me, or should I follow you?"

I don't want to complicate things, so I suggest, "How about if we leave my car here and take yours? That is, if you're cool with driving me back after dinner."

Playfully, she tells me, "As long as you behave, you'll have a ride."

"Oooh…" I pretend to shudder. "Tough talk from such a pretty woman."

"That's right," she warns. "So you'll be good?"

"I promise. I'll be a gem."

"Cool. Now we just need to decide where we should go."

Chapter
ELEVEN

Harder Than I Thought
Becca

After giving Lars a little bit of a hard time—all in fun, of course—I say, "Cool. Now we just need to decide where we should go."

Looking contemplative, but smartass-y as well—no surprise there—he replies, "I think we should go someplace low-key and *friend-like*. We're going to have to think about it. This could take a while."

He's such a snot.

A gorgeous snot, but a snot nonetheless.

Sighing, I remark, "I see you're going to be one of *those* kinds of friends."

"What kind of friend is that?" he asks, grinning over at me. "Would it be the 'hot' kind? Or maybe the 'super-intelligent' kind?"

"My God." I throw my hands up in the air for the second time tonight. "You're impossible. And by the way, you just proved my point. You're clearly the 'difficult' kind of friend."

I don't add that he's right on one count, though—Lars is definitely the hottest friend I've ever had.

He's also the only one I've ever wanted to kiss so badly.

Stop!

I can totally do this friend thing.

After all, it's my idea.

Why did I choose this again?

Ah, yes, I'm protecting my heart.

Wise move, seeing as Lars is total heartbreaker material.

Clearly trying to prove he's not difficult, he comes up with an idea on where we should go. "How about we just grab some pizza and beer somewhere? Is that simple enough for you?"

I frown, glancing down at my dress and then over at him in his suit. "We're a little dressed up for pizza and beer, don't you think?"

He shrugs. "Nah, and who cares, anyway? Let's just do what we want."

"All right, pizza and beer it is." I put the car in gear and add, "Lucky for you, the best pizza shop in all of Columbus is just down the road."

"Cool. I've been trying to find good pizza in this town."

"Then you're going to love this place," I reply.

I turn out of the lot and head down the road to my favorite pizza place in the whole wide world.

"Prepare to be wowed," I tell Lars.

I feel his eyes on me as he murmurs, "It wouldn't be the first time I've been wowed tonight."

"Er... uh..."

Since I'm trying to keep things platonic, I just ignore him and keep on driving.

Secretly, though, I'm melting from his compliment.

When we arrive at the pizza joint, which is an old repurposed warehouse, and head inside, Lars is quickly recognized by several patrons.

Fans rush up to him, asking for autographs.

He signs a few—very graciously, I note—and then the hostess leads us to a private booth in the back.

"I can't believe I didn't realize who you were in the theatre," I remark once we're alone.

"Must've been the ball cap," Lars says. "And it was pretty dark in there."

I tap my menu to my chin. "It wasn't just that. I mean, I watch football and all, but I guess I never really pay attention to the players' faces. The interviews and all that side stuff, I generally tune out. That's more Jodi's vibe."

"Ah." Lars nods. "That makes sense."

Chuckling, I add, "It's also kind of wild you're the football player those two have been trying to set me up with since the fall."

"It is kind of funny," he agrees. "Maybe they know us better than we know ourselves."

We're veering beyond "friends" territory, so I warn, "Lars."

"Okay, okay." He opens his menu and changes the subject. "What should we order? Thin crust, deep dish, toppings, no toppings? This is your favorite pizza place, so it's totally your call."

"Let's go with the deep dish," I say. "It's so good. There are big chunky tomatoes in the sauce and lots of mozzarella cheese. Oh, and speaking of toppings, is just pepperoni okay with you? You'll be able to fully taste the awesomeness of the pizza if we don't overload it with too much."

"Sure. That works for me," Lars says.

Our waitress arrives and we order our pizza, but opt for soft drinks instead of beer, seeing as we both have to drive.

When she leaves, Lars levels me with a look like he's dying to ask me a million questions.

That's fine.

I have some of my own that I'd like to ask—like why must he be so tall, dark, and handsome?

Yeah, no, better to keep that question to myself.

When he continues to just stare over at me, I ask, "What?"

"I was just thinking…" he begins.

"Thinking about what? Do share."

"Well, besides the fact that you're Jodi's best friend and share a business with her, I know almost nothing about you."

"You know I don't pay attention to football players' faces when I'm watching the games."

He chuckles. "Yes, there is that."

"You also know I was born and raised in Columbus."

He sighs. "Yes, and you know I'm from Florida. But what about *you*, Becca? What do you like, besides old movies and deep-dish pizza with pepperoni?"

I want to say "I like you," but that could be misconstrued.

No, it definitely would.

Damn, this is harder than I thought it would be.

But I know I can do it.

I can stay strong, even when faced with the onslaught of Lars's hotness.

Tapping my chin, I murmur, "What do I like, what do I like? Let me think… Oh, I know. I like sushi and fast cars."

"I like those things too," Lars replies with a smile. "But give me something more substantial, something more *you*."

"Besides that I'm stubborn," I tease.

"Yes," he counters quietly, "besides that."

"Okay." I sigh. "I guess if we're truly going to be friends, we need to know each other on a deeper level."

"We do. So spill."

"All right. Well, I like sticking up for my friends. And I like being there for people."

"Those are both great qualities," Lars says softly.

"Like with Jodi," I go on. "She's been my best friend since junior high school. I had her back then, and I still have her back. That's just the way I am—loyal. Jodi's like a sister to me, which is nice since I grew up with a bunch of brothers."

Lars's brows shoot up. "No way. I have a lot of brothers too. How many in your family?"

"Five," I reply. "We're spread out all over nowadays, but we try to get together for family dinners whenever we can."

"Ah, that sounds nice." He nods. "So you're the only girl?"

"Yes."

"Interesting. I have four brothers. No sisters at all."

"Wow, all boys," I remark. "That must've been fun growing up."

"Yeah, it was." He chuckles. "My poor mom, though. We were a handful. Speaking of which, I bet it was an adventure being the only girl in a family with five boys."

Our pizza and soft drinks arrive, and we each grab a slice.

While I wait for mine to cool, I reply, "It was a little crazy with all brothers. The good thing, though, is that they taught me to take care of myself."

Lars pretends to be scared. "Uh-oh, should I be worried?"

Pointing over at him with the pizza slice I just lifted from my plate, I say, "Like I told you earlier, just behave yourself and you'll be fine."

"Noted," he replies, smiling.

We dive into our food then, and I think about how I need to behave too. I have to try and not send Lars mixed signals.

But how am I supposed to do that when I freaking want him so much?

I tell myself I'm just a sucker for a man in a dark suit.

Ah, but we know that's not true.

He looks good in jeans too.

I think about what would happen if I just said "fuck it" and took him to my bed tonight.

What would it be like to feel him slowly peeling off my dress, kissing his way down my body, licking, tasting, touching—

I let out a little gasp.

"Becca?" Lars is peering over at me curiously, one brow raised.

No wonder.

Besides my misplaced gasp, I'm holding a partially eaten slice of pizza halfway to my mouth, staring off into space, thinking lusty thoughts about my *friend*.

The word "friend" flashes in big neon letters in my head as I pull myself together.

"Sorry," I say, while waving around my free hand. "I just spaced for a minute. That's another thing you should know about me. I do that sometimes."

Not a lie, so that's good.

Lars smirks at me while I take a big bite of pizza.

"What?" I mumble around the mouthful.

"Nothing," he says, shaking his head.

Uh oh, I think he knows exactly what was on my mind, or some version of it.

Crap.

This man is far too perceptive. I'm going to have to do a much better job of masking my feelings.

Starting… right… now.

Go!

Chapter
TWELVE

She's Not Fooling Me
Lars

*I*f there's one thing I know besides football, it's women.

That's why Becca is not fooling me one little bit.

Even though she's trying to act all cool and nonchalant, her giveaway gasp and her sitting here lost in thought clues me in.

Yeah, I know she's imagining all the things I could do to her if she were to lose that slinky dress.

I'd help her with that too, slipping my hands up under the fabric, lifting it up.

Fuck, now *my* thoughts are of a sexual nature.

I quickly fix that, though.

Becca wants me friend-zoned, so friend-zoned I shall remain.

See, I can play this game.

Let's see who breaks first.

Becca schools her features to neutral, and things go back to normal. We eat pizza and talk. She asks me a lot about football, including how I like playing for the Comets.

Leaning back and wiping my mouth with a cloth napkin, I say, "It's okay. The guys are great, but our team's not the best in its current state. I hope we can turn things around next season. Not only did we have a losing record this year, but we had a lot of drama with our quarterback."

Becca nods knowingly. "I'm sure you guys will turn things around. A few strategic player changes and the Comets will surely make the playoffs."

"Shit, I hope you're right. That would be amazing."

"Just keep the faith, Lars. Never give up."

"Oh, I won't," I assure her, meeting and holding her gaze. "Not in football… or in any other areas of my life."

I mean her, and she knows it.

Quickly, she looks away.

But even as she does, I detect the tiniest hint of a smile.

Things continue to go well, but we eventually leave the pizza place.

As Becca drives me back to the restaurant parking lot so I can fetch my car, the subject of her work comes up. She tells me how she's hoping to straighten up and organize the wedding consultant bridal shop that she shares with Jodi.

"It's such a mess," she says. "It has been for a while. Our desks are piled high with papers, and the whole space is just so damn unorganized. We recently started carrying wedding dresses, so there are boxes all over the place."

"Sounds like you're expanding," I remark.

"We kind of are. We never planned to get so busy so fast. But business is great."

Chuckling, I say, "That's a good problem to have."

"It sure is. That's why we figured why not strike while the iron's hot and add a product line."

I like that she's not just pretty, she's smart and business-minded.

We arrive at the Italian restaurant and pull into the lot. I direct

Becca over to where my SUV, a black Lincoln Navigator I usually refer to as "the Nav," is parked.

When she pulls in next to my vehicle, I come up with an idea on how I can help Becca *and* be supportive of her business.

As she's placing her car in *Park*, I ask, "Do you and Jodi plan to get things in the shop organized anytime soon?"

Becca sighs. "I'd love to, but I don't think it'll happen as quickly as I'd like."

"Yeah, why's that?"

"Well, we've been talking about organizing since the fall, yet we still haven't made a move. Jodi was supposed to get Caleb to help, but I don't think she ever asked him."

Quickly, I say, "I'll help."

She looks over at me, her eyes lighting up. "Would you really, Lars? That'd be great."

"Yeah, sure," I reply. "In fact, I'd love to help."

Apart from wanting to be a good "friend," I'm up for any opportunity to spend more time with Becca.

She looks super happy, but then her face falls.

"What's up?" I ask.

Sighing, she tells me, "I can't ask you to help with organizing. It'll take hours, maybe even a whole day."

"That's not a problem," I assure her. "My days aren't exactly packed at the moment."

"Ah, right, it's the off-season. I forgot."

"Yeah," I go on, "so you should definitely take me up on my offer while I'm still free."

She cocks her head, smiling. "You really want to help?"

"I do."

"Okay, then let's do it."

"It'll be good," I say. "We'll make it fun."

Before we call it a night, we make a plan for me to meet her at her shop on Sunday morning.

Becca says, "We're closed that day, so that'll work out perfectly."

"Great. I'll see you then," I reply.

I keep it to myself that I'll be counting down the days till Sunday.

Shit, I have to laugh.

Who'd ever expect I'd be this pumped to clean up a bridal shop?

Chapter THIRTEEN

Missing Out

Becca

*L*ars is fantastic. I'm glad we're going to be friends. Grabbing pizza last night with him was so much fun. And now I'm really pumped we'll be spending Sunday together straightening up the shop.

Yay!

It needs to be done, and there's no one else I'd rather do it with.

Come to think of it, there are a lot of things I'd like to do with Lars.

Too bad I can't.

Since I should clear the plan to straighten up the shop with Jodi first, I bring it up to her the next day. We're at our business, seated on the floor in the back by the dressing rooms, unboxing a new line of designer wedding gowns that just came in.

Jodi is one step ahead of me, though, when it comes to Lars.

Seems she wants to talk about nothing but him.

"So where did you guys go last night after you left the restaurant?" she asks as she's opening a huge box of dresses. "When Caleb and I took off, we noticed your car was gone, but Lars's SUV was still there."

"Yeah…" I shrug. "…I drove."

"Where did you go?" Jodi presses. "Did you guys grab something to eat somewhere else?"

"We actually did," I confirm. "We got pizza."

She nods approvingly. "Ahh, something casual. Good thinking. That's less stress than a fancy dinner. I should've suggested that to begin with. Anyway, how did it go?"

"It went great." I start smiling like crazy. I just can't help it. "We got along really well."

Lifting a billowy dress out of a box, Jodi raises a brow. "Does that mean you kissed him again?"

"No!" I grab the dress from her and place it on a hanger. "We decided it's best if we stay friends."

Jodi snorts. "Friends, huh? Is this his idea or yours?"

"It's mine," I snap, huffing.

I'm trying to remain resolute in my decision, but Jodi knows me far too well. Even she can see I'm not thrilled with the direction I'm taking on this.

"Becca," she says on a sigh. "What the hell kind of stupid idea is that? You like Lars, right?" I nod weakly, and she goes on. "I thought so. I mean, clearly you liked him enough to attack him at the movie theatre."

"Hey!"

Jodi ignores me, adding with a sly wink, "You also know for sure now that he's not a serial killer."

"Ha ha." I roll my eyes.

She thinks she's so funny.

But Jodi grows serious when she says, "Come on, Becca. Be honest. What's the real problem here?"

Ugh, I hate that I can never hide anything from her.

But really, I kind of do want to talk about my misgivings with someone.

After all, she is my best friend.

"Okay, here goes nothing." Placing my head in my hands, I admit, "The fact that there is no problem *is* the problem."

"Huh?" I look up to find Jodi frowning. "What does that even mean, you goofball?"

"It means I want to protect my heart, okay? Lars is a gorgeous pro football player. He can have anyone he wants."

"But he wants you," Jodi states quietly.

I shake my head. "No, he just wants to fuck me at this point. I'm sure that's the truth of it. He doesn't know me well enough to want me for me."

I know I have her there, so I underline my point by standing and forcefully hanging up the dress I've been clutching onto. I place a plastic covering over the damn thing, rather noisily, to add exclamation to what I'm saying.

By the time I sit back down on the floor, Jodi is staring at me concernedly.

"What?" I ask. "Why are you looking at me like that?"

"You know, you're scaring me," she says, leaning back on one of the unopened boxes. "I don't want to see you missing out."

"Missing out?" I chortle. "Yeah, right. Missing out on heartbreak and despair? Yeah, no, I think I'll pass."

"Becca, it's not heartbreak and despair I'm talking about. Sure, there's always a chance you could get hurt. It's that way for everyone when you open yourself up to love. But what I'm talking about is something else entirely, something applicable to you in this situation."

"Jeez, you're so dramatic." I blow out a breath. "Enlighten me, Jodi, please. What am I potentially missing out on?"

Holding my gaze, she says, "Possibility, Becca. You could be missing out on real possibility."

Shit, she's got me there.

Chapter FOURTEEN

Drowning in Dresses
Lars

*B*y two o'clock on Sunday afternoon, I'm fucking drowning in wedding dresses. I've never seen so much lace and silk and something Becca tells me is called "tulle."

What the fuck is tulle?

Of course, she finds all of this hilarious.

Laughing, as she stands above where I'm seated on the floor of her shop, surrounded by mounds of wedding gowns, she says, "I should grab my phone and take a picture of this."

"Don't you dare," I warn.

"Aw, come on. We could put it on your Instagram and title it 'Marriage Material.'"

Whoa, what?

We look at each other.

Becca is blushing like crazy.

But I start smiling.

"Thanks for the compliment," I say.

Scrambling to recover from her faux pas, she says, "Er, uh, I was only trying to think of something witty."

Yeah, sure you were.

That's okay.

Let her play it cool.

When I try to catch her gaze, Becca pretends to be deeply interested in a tag on a dress.

Stirring the pot a little, I ask, "Whatcha looking at?"

Still examining the tag, even more closely now, she mumbles, "I'm just checking out the SKU number. I think this one is wrong."

Ha, yeah right.

I bet you a million dollars it's fine.

But, whatever.

I drop the subject and let her check out the supposedly incorrect tag in peace.

She looks so cute standing there in her tight blue jeans and black hoodie over a white tee, pretending to be preoccupied. There's a hint of pink shading her cheeks, making her even more desirable.

Damn it.

If we weren't "just friends," I'd pull her down onto these dresses and do unspeakable things to her right the hell on top of the fucking "tulle."

But, as she so often likes to remind me, we're just buds.

Clearing my throat in an effort to garner her attention, I let Becca in on a secret. "Hey, just for the record, I actually don't have an Instagram account."

She lets go of the tag and folds the dress over her arm. "You don't?"

"Nope."

"Well, we definitely need to remedy that."

Wait, whoa, what?

"Uh, I don't think so," I state firmly. "I like my privacy far too much."

Tossing the billowy dress at me—of course I catch it—she says, "You're no fun."

"That's it." I stand, dropping the dress and stepping out of the mound of tulle hell. "No fun, you say?" I raise a challenging brow. "I'm about to show you how much fun I am."

I lunge for her, but she's quicker than I anticipate, spinning around and doing what Becca Nadeau does best—running away.

Chapter FIFTEEN

Running Still, but Slowing Down
Becca

I run from Lars.

I'm so good at this.

I have an advantage too, since we're in my store and I know where to hide.

Hiding is another one of my specialties.

Scampering to a storeroom that's down a short hall, I rush inside the small space, slamming the door behind me and locking it.

Just in the nick of time too.

Lars is on my ass.

Had he caught me, who knows what I would've done?

I could have lost my resolve.

I mean, damn, he looks sexier than ever today in his dark jeans and black and red flannel shirt he has on over a gray pullover.

Good thing I made it to this storeroom.

I don't care what Jodi says. Possibility or not, I'm playing it on the safe side.

Knocking on the door, Lars calls out, "Hey, no fair. You can't lock yourself away from me."

"Yes, I can," I retort.

There's a pause, and then Lars, in a much softer voice, says, "Becca, what do you think would happen if I were to catch you?"

"Nothing," I lie.

In my head, I'm confronted with the truth.

I think you would kiss me.

And I'd let you.

I'd like it too.

And then our whole friends-only pact would shatter.

Jodi and her good advice be damned, I can't let that happen.

Clearing my throat, I try to make a joke. "Hey, bud," I warn, leaning against the door. "I'm competitive like you, meaning I'm all about winning. Letting you catch me would equate to surrender."

I swear I hear him murmur, "You may like surrendering to me, Becca."

Damn, would he just stop?

Sighing, I call out, "If I open the door, are you going to be good?"

"That depends on your definition of good."

"Lars..."

"Yes, yes, okay." I hear him blow out a long breath. "I'll be an angel."

When I open the door, he's making a little halo circle above his head.

Pushing him out of the way—*hey, any excuse to allow me to touch that hard bod of his*—I say, "Smartass. Now let's get back to work on those dresses."

In the days and weeks that follow our Sunday spent cleaning and straightening up the wedding consultant shop, my friendship with Lars really begins to blossom.

We somehow manage to put our attraction on the back burner, meaning we focus solely on getting to know one another.

I visit his home, which is freaking large and impressive, a suburban stone monstrosity, and he comes over to my much more modest tiny blue frame house in the country. At both our homes, we binge-watch shows on Netflix, and he shows me highlight films from last season.

Even though the Comets had a losing record, they won a couple of their final games. They had a backup quarterback at the helm by that point, but Lars still played phenomenally.

One highlight he shows me has him turning and catching a forty-yard pass as he's running up the field.

I watch with bated breath, scooting to the edge of his buttery soft leather sofa, just as Lars runs into the end zone for a touchdown.

"Woohoo." I raise my arm and pump my fist in the air like the game's going on right now. "Way to go. That was the last thirty seconds of the fourth quarter."

"It was," he modestly agrees.

Patting his knee, I state, "Well, then you saved the game. Good job."

Lars shrugs and looks down at my hand.

I yank it back, and he pretends to brush away imaginary lint from his jeans.

He is so cute.

Usually it's me blushing, but now it's him.

"I was just doing my job," he mutters humbly.

I chortle, "You did more than that. You totally won that game for the Comets."

Quietly, he says, "I guess."

I scoot closer and nudge his arm with mine. "Hey, no guessing about it, okay?"

Staying close like this, we watch more game footage.

I actually enjoy myself more than I expect too. And I pay more attention to the players' faces, especially Lars's.

A few days later, I ask him if we can watch more games.

"I like watching you play," I bravely admit.

He raises a brow. "You do?"

I nod. "Yes, very much."

He looks so pleased as we settle in on his sofa like we did the other night. "Then, sure. Let's do it."

He queues up a game.

And I watch and watch…

A short while later, after observing how consistently freaking amazing Lars is, I ask him, "Why don't you play in the NFL?"

From a few feet away on the sofa, he shrugs. "I don't know. I guess because I'm twenty-nine, and the NFL views me as a little too old to start over."

"That's crazy. Though…" I eye him saucily. "You are four years older than me. That kind of does make you a bit over the hill."

Holding my gaze intently, he says silkily, "I'm hardly over the hill, babe. Though I'm sure I'm far more experienced than the guys you usually, uh, hang out with."

Gulp.

I know exactly what he means by "far more experienced" and "hang out with."

His deep brown eyes scorch into me, and I have to look away.

Quickly, I change the subject.

And so it goes…

When I'm over at Lars's house, or when he's at mine, we don't just watch TV. Sometimes we sit and talk for hours. We're stuck inside for now, but I tell him I can't wait for the weather to get nice so we can hang out on my back porch.

"It's really peaceful and quiet back there," I explain. "That's one advantage to living off the beaten path."

"Indeed it is," he agrees. "I look forward to it."

Spring get here soon!

On the nights we're together, once in a while we drink a couple of beers or hard seltzers. I try to keep my imbibing to a minimum, though, since it lowers my inhibitions. I find myself all too often wanting to reenact our theatre make-out session. That's even when I'm sober. But if I'm tipsy, it's all I can do not to jump the man.

Too bad that can never happen again.

I don't think it will, anyway.

Lars is so well-behaved these days.

Well, for the most part.

He does sometimes say things laden with innuendo.

Still, I don't want to be the one to blow it.

That's why I start thinking maybe we should go out more often. Hanging around in my house and his, with our bedrooms so near, is too tempting.

At this point, for me more than for him.

Help!

We definitely need to get out more.

So when Lars comes up with a road trip idea, I'm all in.

Excitedly, I ask, "Where should we go?"

We're in his living room, and as he leans back on the sofa next to the chair I'm seated in, he says, "I was looking online the other day and I noticed Niagara Falls isn't all that far from here. Have you ever been there?"

I shake my head. "No, but you do realize the falls are not all that close? It takes about five hours by car to get there."

Leveling me with a you're-no-fun roll of his eyes, Lars says, "Isn't that the point of a road trip? Getting there is half the fun."

"Getting there will take up a lot of time," I counter.

I want to go, but I just want him to realize it's no quick trip.

Good thing he is in no way discouraged. "Ah, who cares if it takes a while? We can leave early in the morning, drive up to the area, and spend a few hours checking out the falls. It sounds like a great way to spend the day, if you ask me."

He does kind of have a point. Plus, again, I'd like nothing more than to spend several hours seated next to Lars, driving up to Niagara Falls and back.

I nod. "Yeah, I think it's doable. Let's go for it."

"That's the spirit," Lars exclaims.

"There is something to consider, though," I warn.

"Yeah, what's that?"

"It is still March. There aren't going to be a lot of places that are open up there. And it may be kind of chilly."

"Who cares?" Lars says. "I just want to see the falls. I don't mind if it's not warm. That is"—he raises a brow—"if you're okay with that."

I roll my eyes at him. "I'm fine with chilly weather. I live in Ohio, don't I?"

"Ah, yes, you do. But as I recall, you once told me how much you hate snow. I'm assuming that includes the cold."

Ah, so he does remember what I said that night in the theatre.

Smiling, I tell him, "You are absolutely right about me hating snow and being cold. That's why I plan to check the forecast religiously before we go. I'm going to make sure it's A-okay for a day trip."

That makes Lars laugh. "I'm sure you'll do that, Becca. I'm sure you will."

He already knows me so well.

Eek, that's a little scary.

But I'm not running.

Chapter SIXTEEN

Road Trip

Lars

Becca and I pick a day for our Niagara Falls adventure. She's calling it that now, and I'm happy to go along with it.

I hope it is an adventure, a great one.

We end up choosing the last Friday in March. She's not working at the consultant shop that day, and hell, I can take time off from working out anytime I want.

Becca, as I knew she would, checks the weather faithfully in the days leading up to our trip.

All is good, meaning there's no snow in the forecast and no frigid cold.

With the plan on, I pick her up early Friday morning at her house.

As she hops into the Navigator, she asks, "You have your passport, right?"

I reply, "I sure do."

"Good." She nods approvingly. "We're still in great shape with the weather too. There could be some light rain showers off and on, but the temperature is supposed to hover in the low fifties."

Laughing, I say, "Thank you for that weather report. Do you have a traffic update too?"

"Ha, ha, Lars. You're so funny."

She smacks my arm as I place the car in gear.

"Seriously, though," I go on, "that sounds great. It won't be freezing cold or pouring snow. And"—I nod down to the jeans, hiking boots, dark long-sleeved tee, and olive green rain jacket I'm wearing—"I came prepared for rain."

"I did too," Becca says, smiling as she gestures to her own attire.

After I turn around in her long driveway, I stop the vehicle and take a look.

She is indeed ready for rain, having on pretty much the same style of clothes I have on: a rain jacket—though hers is black, not green—hiking boots, a long-sleeved tee, and jeans.

Her jeans are of the skinny variety, and I can't help but notice how they accentuate her curves in a way that makes me have to look away.

If Becca catches me, she'll see the want and longing in my eyes.

I'm trying to play it cool, be her "friend."

Oh, hell.

"We better get going." I blow out a breath as I hit the gas. "We have a long drive ahead of us."

I'm worried that trying not to think dirty thoughts about Becca when she's sitting this close to me for the next five hours may prove a challenge. I've already had one lusty thought and we're only just now heading away from her house.

I've been so good lately too, keeping my innuendo and flirting to a minimum.

You can do this, I remind myself.

I can.

I got this.

I so very much do.

As we travel through the state of Ohio, I keep our conversation strictly platonic.

Becca does too.

She tells me more details about her life growing up in Columbus. And I share info with her about my younger years in Florida.

"I had a lot of friends in the neighborhood I grew up in. That made it really easy to put together ragtag football games with me and my brothers. We did that pretty much all the time."

"No wonder you're so good," Becca remarks.

I smile over at her before returning my eyes to the road. "Thanks for saying that."

"It's true, Lars. Watching all those highlights and games from the end of the Comets season last year showed me one thing."

I'm curious, so I ask, "Yeah? What's that?"

"It proves you weren't the problem with the team."

"No." I blow out a breath. "I guess not. I played pretty well as an individual. But, as you know, it takes a whole team to win. Sadly, our defense was consistently weak, and the quarterback we had for most of the season was absolutely horrible."

Becca sighs. "Yeah, I heard about him. He was a real jerk and kind of a nut."

I chuckle. "That's putting it mildly."

"Good thing he's gone, yeah?"

"Yeah, good thing."

I shake my head, thinking of the details of the sordid quarterback mess. It's a long story, but suffice it to say that life with the QB we once dubbed Dumbo was not a fun time for the team.

Becca, nodding contemplatively and clearly having learned the details from Jodi, asks, "What do you think the Comets are planning to do about this upcoming season? I heard they're shopping around for a new starting quarterback. Is that true?"

"Yes." I nod. "Our backup is okay, but he's not starting material. There's chatter that the Comets are looking real hard at a guy named

Graham Tettersaw."

"Huh, is that so? Is he any good?"

"He is," I confirm. "But we'll see what happens. It's too early for any major moves."

We talk some more about random stuff, until we reach the New York state line.

Excited, I point over to a huge sign on the side of the road welcoming incoming travelers. "Ah, we have officially reached New York. It won't be long now till we're at our destination."

"It won't," Becca agrees, sounding pumped. "I can't believe how quickly the time's going by."

Glancing over at her, I say softly, "Must be the good company, huh?"

She laughs. "Yes, and that goes both ways."

She's such a doll.

We continue traveling north on I-90. I can't believe I'm having such a good time just driving. I swear I could do anything with Becca and have a blast.

When we find ourselves closing in on Buffalo, she says, "Should we grab some lunch before we're at Niagara Falls?"

"Absolutely," I reply, my stomach concurring with a loud rumble. "I thought you'd never ask."

Snickering, she says, "Yes. It sounds like someone's hungry."

I protest, "Hey, it's past noon. We've been on the road for quite a while. This big body requires a lot of nourishment."

I catch her glancing over at me, her gaze traveling up my legs, over my torso, and to my face.

Pretending I haven't noticed a thing, I return my eyes to the road. I won't bust her.

But her perusal does make me feel happy.

I'm glad I'm not the only one always throwing out hungry glances.

And I'm about to do more, when, out of the corner of my eye, I catch her licking her lips. I almost freaking let out a groan.

Shit, I need to get my mind back on the subject at hand—food.

Thank God there's a big green-and-white road sign up ahead.

Pointing to it, I say, "Hey, there's an exit coming up. We can get something to eat there."

"Sounds good," Becca says. "Let's do it."

"Let's," I agree.

We bump fists, perfectly too, like we've been doing this song and dance for years.

Fuck, we really have become good friends.

We're synchronized in clothing and in actions.

Why does that make me feel so damn good?

I don't know, and I don't have time to process it.

I take the next exit, as planned, and we immediately come upon a string of restaurants.

Though the choices are many, we opt for something quick and easy—burgers and fries from a fast food joint.

It's not gourmet cuisine, but it does the trick.

A short while later, we finally reach our destination—Niagara Falls.

After parking and buying a guide book from a gift shop, Becca and I find ourselves standing on an observation deck on the Canadian side, checking out the amazing views.

"I think I like this vantage point best," Becca says, holding up her phone and snapping a photo.

"It is amazing," I concur as I do the same.

She then steps back from the railing.

Paging through the guide book, she says, "It says here that these are called Horseshoe Falls."

"I can see why," I reply. "They're shaped like one."

Leaning over the railing, I take more pics with my phone.

Becca slides in next to me, and since she's standing really fucking close, the electricity that is always there but is usually kept at bay roars to life.

She must feel it too, as she quickly steps away, putting some space between us.

"Damn, I was just about to suggest a selfie," I joke.

Looking flustered, she says, "Um, we can still take one."

She stands beside me once more, though not as close, and I snap a selfie of us.

Moving away swiftly, she says, "See, if you were on Instagram, you could post that picture."

I check out the photo and realize that though we're not all jammed up on each other, we look like a couple, one with deep feelings for each other.

Showing Becca the pic, I poignantly state, "I'm fine with keeping this one all for myself."

"Mmm, yeah…"

She walks away, pretending to be immersed in the brochure.

Hey, at least she's not running.

When she turns back around, she says, "We should check out some other viewing points. This brochure has a long list of places to stop and take photos."

"Sure." I nod. "Let's do it."

Despite my enthusiastic tone, a part of me feels sad. I'm starting to really dislike this friends-only crap. It gets harder every day for me to pretend like I'm not attracted to Becca, insanely attracted to her. Not to mention, my feelings for her have grown stronger as I've gotten to know her.

I really care about this girl.

But what can I do?

This is how she wants us to be—friends only.

Sighing resignedly, I hold out my arm. "Okay, lead the way."

I follow Becca to the next great viewing point, just as I will continue to follow her in the path of this relationship.

For some reason, though, I have a strong suspicion there's about to be a detour.

Chapter
SEVENTEEN

No, Not Snow!
Becca

*T*his day is turning out to be so much fun and much more than I expected. I knew Lars and I would have a good time, as we always do, but this is next level.

I guess it was good to get away.

One thing, it's giving me a new perspective on things.

I enjoyed the drive up to New York and Canada with Lars, and I've absolutely loved checking out Niagara Falls with him. But I've realized something, something I've been running from.

Despite all my friends-only rules, I've slowly been falling for Lars Samuels.

As in, I love him.

There's no denying there's just something really fantastic between us. It's more than just how well we get along, which is amazing. But friendship aside, that sexual energy that's been there from the start has only grown stronger.

That's why I *had* to move away from him on the observation

deck. Otherwise, I might have done something foolish.

And now he wants a selfie.

I stand a reasonable distance away as he snaps the pic. I then crack a joke about Instagram and how he could post the photo if he had an account.

And then he shows me the selfie.

Damn, we look like a couple in love.

I quickly turn my attention to the guide book, and soon we move to a different viewing spot.

Only problem is, even though I'm standing a few safe feet away, the pull is still there, urging me to close the gap.

Oh, what the hell.

The fight in me is waning.

I inch a little closer to Lars, testing the waters.

But before I can gauge whether this is a wise move or not, my whole plan is washed out, like literally, when it starts to rain.

Damn it!

It's not just a shower; it's a freaking deluge.

"Shit, crap." I yank my jacket hood up over my head, not that it helps much.

Lars does the same, hollering over the pounding rain, "I thought only light showers were in the forecast."

As we desperately glance left and right, seeking some kind of shelter, I yell back, "Clearly the weather people were wrong."

Laughing, he remarks, "Isn't that usually the case?"

Spotting an open cafe around the corner, I point in that direction and say, "Should we head over there?"

"Absolutely," Lars replies.

We make a run for it.

Once we're inside the cafe, shaking rainwater from our jackets, he says, "This looks like a good spot to wait out this storm."

"Definitely." I pull my hood down, running my fingers through my damp hair. "I think this is perfect. We can even get something warm to drink."

"Sounds good," he says.

We find two seats at the counter and, when the waitress comes by, we order two hot coffees.

While we're waiting, I take out my phone and check for updates on the weather.

Once I read the forecast, I murmur, "Crap."

"What's wrong?" Lars asks.

In a tone filled with pure dread, I reply, "Snow. Snow is on the way."

The coffees arrive, and he holds up his cup.

As he's about to take a sip, he says, "Wait. I thought the temps were staying in the fifties."

"Ah, that's obviously changed." I turn the phone around so Lars can see the bad news for himself.

"Fuck," he grinds out.

Turning the phone back my way, I say, "I better turn on the alerts. I could've caught this had I done so earlier. Anyway, here's the full forecast. The temperature is falling. It should drop into the low thirties within the next hour." I look over at him. "That means this rain will turn to snow real freaking soon."

Frowning but still looking gorgeous, especially with how his dark hair is all messy and damp, Lars says, "I suck at driving in the snow. I'm a Florida guy, meaning I've not had much experience."

"I can drive," I offer. "But I must warn you, I'm not the best snow-driver either, seeing as I try to stay out of the white stuff as much as possible."

Setting his cup down with a clink, he says, "This sucks, Becca. I hate having to leave already. It feels like we just got here. Still, I think the wisest course of action is to hit the road as soon as we can and head back to Ohio."

"Yeah, I agree. With this kind of weather moving in, it'll get dark real fast. And that always makes everything worse."

With the decision made, we finish our coffees quickly and leave the cafe.

It's noticeably colder when we step outside. It's still raining, though much more lightly than before. There is a different feel to it, though, which concerns me.

"We really need to get out of here," I warn. "I think that snow is arriving sooner rather than later."

Lars nods. "It would seem so."

We retrieve the SUV from where we parked and prepare to start on our way back home. I offer to drive again, but Lars insists he's got it for now since we're only dealing with rain.

I'm cool with that.

But a short while later, once we're in New York state, traveling south on I-90, the rain turns to something far worse than snow—it turns to freaking freezing rain.

"This is awful," I squeak out, my heart pounding. "It feels like it's already super slippery."

"It is," Lars confirms. "I have traction control on, but it's not helping much."

I blow out a stuttered breath. "You know, I really think we should get off the highway and stop for a while. Freezing rain is a whole other animal than snow."

Lars is up for stopping, no surprise there. It'd be crazy to continue.

"I see an exit up ahead," he says. "We can get off there."

Relieved, I breathe out a fast, "That sounds perfect."

My phone dings, indicating there's a new weather alert.

When I check it, I find confirmation that this is only the beginning of the freezing rain. It's going to last for a while before turning to just snow.

This is bad.

"I don't even see any salt trucks out here," I say, panicked, as we proceed down the exit ramp cautiously. "There's really no one out at all."

Oh, boy.

If people in upstate New York are staying in, the weather really must be bad.

Sighing, I lament, "Maybe we better think about finding a place to stay for the night."

Raking his fingers through his hair, Lars concedes, "That's not a bad idea."

The only problem is the exit we've just taken is leading us into bumfuck nowhere. The road we end up turning onto is a country lane, surrounded by nothing but fields and farms.

We look at each other with concern.

"This doesn't look promising," I state direly.

Lars mutters, "No, it doesn't."

Luckily, as we drive slowly down the slippery road, a billboard for an old motor lodge motel comes into view.

Pointing, I say, "Phew! We might be in luck after all."

Lars breathes a visible sigh of relief.

Crap, I feel the same.

"I can't really make out the name of the motel," I say, squinting to see through the freezing rain that is pelting the windshield even with the wipers working overtime.

Visibility is bad enough, but the sign is sun-faded and weather-worn.

Still, I tell Lars, "It does say 'motel,' and it's up the road just another mile. Let's go for it."

"Definitely," he agrees. "We'll check it out."

We make our way along the road slowly, the wiry branches of the trees sheathed in ice.

When it starts to get really slick, we slow to a crawl. Not simply to be safe but to make sure we don't miss the entrance to the motel.

"Wait, that's our turn," I say, gesturing to a break in the trees. "There's a smaller sign there, but it's too far back for me to see what it says."

"That's okay. That has to be it," Lars says. "We'll turn in here."

I'm pumped we'll be out of this horrible weather soon. It's far too dangerous to keep driving.

Once we turn into the motel entrance, we park next to the old dilapidated sign that I couldn't make out from the road.

But I see it now. It's flashing out a slow beat of neon pink letters. Pink letters that spell out the name of the motel we're about to rent a room in—The Love Nest.

I try not to laugh.

Great, just what we need.

We've been trying to fight our feelings all damn day. I have a feeling staying here might turn out to be more dangerous than the icy roads.

Yet I'm not running.

Not because there's nowhere to go, but because I want to stay with Lars.

I'm finally ready to be brave and embrace whatever this night holds.

Chapter
EIGHTEEN

The Love Nest
Lars

You have got to be kidding me.

I shake my head.

It's like the fates are against us.

Or maybe they're actually for us, and that's why they're pushing us together.

Why else would the only motel in this godforsaken part of the state be called The Love Nest?

Heaven help us.

I notice Becca is trying not to laugh.

Clearly, she feels pretty much the same way I do.

How could she not?

If the name alone isn't a strong indicator that this is a hookup motel, the bubblegum-pink wooden trim on the low red brick building is a dead giveaway that this place is all about "love."

"Well, at least it seems they keep the place up," Becca states encouragingly, nodding as she glances around. "That's a good sign, right?"

"Yeah," I agree. "It's clearly not a fleabag motel."

It's not.

It's just a little heavy on the pink.

As we pull into a parking spot in front of the motel office on the far end of the building, I point to several cut-out foil hearts adorning the window and murmur, "I can't wait to see what it looks like inside."

"Right? This should be an interesting experience."

I remind Becca, "You know, it could be worse."

Peering over at me curiously, she asks, "How do you mean?"

Tapping the steering wheel absently, I reply, "Well, it's not the motel in the movie *Psycho*. You've seen that, right? Good ole Norman Bates."

"Eek." Becca shudders. "Yes, I've seen the movie. And it would definitely be awful if this place turned out to be anything like that."

Nodding to the hearts on the window again, I say, "Nah, I think we're safe."

With a final thank-God-for-that look from Becca, we hop out of the Nav.

Even though the sidewalk appears to have been heavily salted, I hold Becca's arm as we head into the motel office, which ends up looking a lot like Cupid's den of love.

Letting go of her arm, I take in everything, as does she.

How could you not?

The office is quite the sight.

The wallpaper is a display of pink, red, and purple hearts, arrows, and various depictions of Cupid himself. The carpeting is a deep red, and there's a big pink wicker basket containing candy hearts over on the counter.

"It's kind of funny how we just can't get away from Valentine's Day," Becca remarks as she steps over to the counter and grabs a handful of hearts.

She gives me one, which I place in my jacket pocket.

"Yeah," I reply, chuckling. "Clearly, we can't."

I'm beginning to wonder if it's such a bad thing to be reminded of Valentine's Day. Becca and I never talk about that night, not anymore. We don't ever even make reference to it.

I guess it's just safer that way.

Still, there's no denying The Love Nest is triggering memories.

I know for her too, seeing as she's eyeing me curiously.

When I raise a brow, she quickly looks away.

"Uh," Becca mumbles, "do you want more candy hearts?"

Nice change of subject.

Smiling at her, I reply, "No thanks."

"Okay." She nods. "I'll hold onto the rest for now. They could be our only provisions for the night."

Hmm, she does have a point.

Based on how the icy rain is making a noisy clatter as it hits the roof, those candy hearts may truly be our only source of sustenance for the immediate future.

"Good thing we ate a big lunch," I say.

"Right?"

No one is at the front desk, or coming to it, so I tap the little silver bell on the counter.

"My goodness, sounds like I have a customer," a voice groggily proclaims from the back room, as if the person has just woken up.

Within seconds, a little white-haired lady emerges from the back, patting her bun and stifling a yawn.

I can't blame her for napping. It's not exactly like business is booming in the icy rain.

"I didn't realize someone had come in," she says apologetically. "I'm sorry to keep you waiting. It's just that we don't get much business this time of year. Now on Valentine's Day…" She grins. "It's a whole different story."

"I bet," Becca murmurs.

Thumbing toward the door, I say, "It's a little rough out there with the ice, so we decided to stop and get a room for the night."

The motel lady nods. "That's a very wise choice, sir. You don't want to be out in this mess."

"No, no we don't," Becca concurs.

I pull out my wallet so I can give the lady a credit card, which she runs through.

Becca offers to give me some cash to chip in for the cost, but I tell her, "Don't be silly. I got this. Besides, you're providing the food." I nod to her jacket pocket, where she stashed the hearts.

She winks at me, murmuring, "Ah, yes. There is that."

The motel lady finishes checking us in and hands me the room key, which is an actual metal key on a chain.

"I put you in room fourteen," she says. "Once you go back out, turn left. Your unit is about halfway down the walkway."

"Great, thanks," I say, glancing down at the old-style key.

It's not the red heart keychain that grabs my attention, though that does stand out. Still, no, it's the observation that we're in room fourteen that has me shaking my head.

The Valentine's Day reminders continue.

When I tune back in, the motel lady is informing us that there are vending machines on the other side of the motel, and that she keeps them fully stocked.

"Guess we'll have more than just candy hearts to sustain us after all," Becca says quietly, leaning into me.

Softly, I agree, "Yeah, it looks that way."

Her closeness doesn't go unnoticed. There's a hitch in my throat and a longing to wrap my arm around her shoulders.

But I keep it together and just say, "We better go to our room. It sounds like it's getting worse out there."

And it does.

The pounding on the roof is picking up in intensity.

Since Becca and I don't have luggage to retrieve, we head straight to room number fourteen.

I'm expecting a lot of pink and red inside, a continuation of the "love" theme, to remind us of Valentine's Day. But when we turn on the light, we discover there's an even bigger problem.

"Uh oh," Becca says. "There's only one bed."

"And it's covered in pink satin sheets and shaped like a fucking heart," I blurt out. "You have got to be kidding me."

Misunderstanding my frustration, she turns to me and says softly, "I can stay on my side, Lars. I promise."

It's not her I'm worried about.

"No." I shake my head. "I'll just sleep on the floor. You take the bed."

"Don't be ridiculous." She frowns as she peers down at the threadbare faded red carpeting. "This floor looks really uncomfortable. Just sleep in the bed with me."

"Becca…"

Giving me a stern look, she says, "Lars, stop. We got this. We're not children."

"Yeah, that's what I'm afraid of."

Can we really spend the whole night in a bed together with nothing happening?

A bed that's heart-shaped and covered in pink satin.

In a motel named The Love Nest.

One thing for sure, this is shaping up to be our biggest challenge yet.

Chapter NINETEEN

Temptation

Becca

*H*mm, this should be interesting... and definitely not easy.

Lars and I have to sleep in a heart-shaped bed, surrounded by themes of love and reminders of our Valentine's Day make-out session. The one we're not supposed to allow happen again.

How am I supposed to stay strong?

Do I even want to anymore?

I can't help but think how much fun it'd be to let go and give in to my feelings, especially now that Lars and I have an actual friendship. There's not just a strong attraction between us, there's a growing need for more—a very palpable need.

Even though we don't discuss it, it's there.

Yes, how many times have I found myself checking out his firm ass, admiring his broad shoulders and wide chest, and drooling over his defined muscles?

The answer is *a lot.*

I haven't even gotten to Lars's face, which is so nice to look at.

I peer over at his full lips now, remembering how they felt pressed to mine.

So good, so very good. Soft, yet firm and forceful.

Gah!

I tell Lars that "we got this," but do we?

I hope he does, because my resolve is definitely crumbling.

Maybe it's because of all these hearts everywhere?

Or maybe it's due to the love theme in general?

It could also be that Lars and I had such a fun day, despite the freezing rain ruining our plans.

I don't know.

Maybe this is better.

Maybe this is meant to be.

Should I keep denying that I freaking want him to hold me in his arms?

Or, more precisely, that I want him to hold me down on this stupid heart-shaped bed and touch me like I know he can.

I'm tired of kidding myself.

What I want is for him to fu—

"Becca? Becca, are you all right? You look really out of it right now. Maybe you need something to eat, something more substantial than candy?"

Yeah, I need you.

Oh, I can't say that.

Lars is clearly perplexed as to why I'm standing here seemingly lost in thought.

Tell him, Becca.

Tell him you're not fine.

Tell him you need his big, hard—

Brrrinnggg!

I almost jump out of my skin as the old landline phone on the nightstand rings, saving me from having to explain.

I have literally just been saved by the bell.

Phew!

The reprieve gives me time to pull my shit together.

As Lars walks over to the nightstand, I pop a candy heart into my mouth, just to put *something* there.

If it can't be Lars, the next best thing is something loaded with sugar.

I watch as Lars answers the phone, talks for a minute, then hangs up.

"Who was it?" I ask.

"It was the lady from the front desk. She wanted to let us know she'll be staying in the office all night long, in case we need anything. I guess it's too bad out for her to drive home."

"Okay," I reply. "That was nice of her to tell us."

"It was," he agrees.

We're just making idle conversation, both of us trying so damn hard not to stare at the heart-shaped bed.

I finally turn away and get to work on finally discarding my soggy jacket and boots.

Lars comes over to the door to do the same.

Afterward, we just kind of stand silently, not knowing what to do next.

Biting my lip, lest I say something that may get me into trouble—like "let's try out that bed"—I lean over to where my jacket is draped over one of two chairs pushed under a small table and reach into the pocket.

"You want some hearts?" I ask Lars as I grab a few.

Shaking his head, he says, "No, I'm good. I am a little thirsty, though."

Ha, I bet.

He's probably having the same lusty thoughts as me.

I gesture to the door. "We can go check out the vending machines, if you want."

"Or…" He points to a mini-bar in the corner that I hadn't even noticed. "We can see what's in there."

"Wow, I didn't even see that," I say. "But yeah, let's check it out. I'm game."

Turns out, the mini-bar is stocked with one thing only—mini bottles of alcohol. And not just any alcohol—champagne.

Lars, kneeling as he holds open the door of the mini-bar, looks up at me and raises a brow.

I just laugh. "We should've known."

"For sure. So"—he points inside—"would you like your own sample size of bubbly?"

I shrug. "You know what? I think I would."

He hands me one of the small bottles of champagne, grabs one for himself, and then stands.

"We have the makings of a real party here," he teases, raising his bottle to tap to mine.

After "clink-ing" my bottle to his, I unscrew the cap.

"It's the fancy stuff, I see," I tease, as it is so not.

That makes Lars laugh. "Yeah, right."

I then proclaim, "Candy and champagne. Who could ask for anything more?"

Flopping down on the bed, Lars says, "We're living the good life here, babe. No doubt about it."

Whoa, I like how he just called me "babe."

I sit down on the edge of the bed, mindful to leave plenty of room between us.

Holding my bottle aloft, I say, "Here's to being snowed in."

He taps my champagne with his bottle, and adds, "Or rather, here's to being frozen in, as it stands for now."

"Good point," I murmur.

We drink champagne and share a few candy hearts. But then we realize we're still really hungry.

"Woman, or man, cannot live on sugar alone," I declare.

"Definitely not," Lars says, standing. "How about if I go rustle us up some grub from the vending machines?"

"Sounds like a plan," I reply, laughing at his playfulness.

"Any requests, m'lady?"

Rolling onto my stomach and peering up at him, I say, "No. Surprise me."

After putting his jacket and boots back on, Lars announces, "I'll be right back."

"Be careful walking out there," I warn, turning serious. "The rock salt from earlier has probably been covered up. The walkway could be really slippery."

"Don't worry," he assures me. "I'll be fine."

Once Lars leaves, I jump up to see if there are more candy hearts in my jacket, even though I'm pretty sure we polished them off.

But no, score!

I find one lonely candy wedged way deep down in the pocket.

"Yes!" I pump my fist, victorious.

Hey, it's the small things.

I realize then that with all the candy hearts Lars and I devoured while we were drinking champagne, we paid no attention to any of the messages printed on them.

I decide to check the message on this last one.

I look down, and two words etched in the candy catch my eye... and my heart.

You're His

The thing of it is I've finally accepted that I really, truly want to be.

Chapter TWENTY

Love Her
Lars

The trek to the vending machines isn't too bad. The motel lady must've come out and laid down a second layer of rock salt, as the ice is melted to mostly slush.

And from above, the freezing rain has changed over to snow.

It's not just a tiny bit, either.

This is like a full-on blizzard.

Becca and I are not only frozen in, we're now officially snowed in.

"She is going to just love this," I murmur, chuckling when I think of how she feels about the white stuff.

Somehow, though, I think she may like it today.

When I reach the vending machines, I fish around in my jacket pocket for coins that I know I have.

I do eventually dig out a few quarters, but I also find something else—the candy heart Becca gave to me back in the motel office.

"Cool, a snack."

Just as I'm about to pop the thing into my mouth, I decide to read the message.

Out loud, I say the words: *Love Her.*

Whoa, what?

I read it again to make sure I'm seeing it correctly.

Yep, it says *Love Her.*

This must be some kind of custom heart. Aren't the messages on these things usually like *Be Mine*?

I bet the motel lady orders these to offer something different and unique for her guests.

But does the message mean something more for me?

Was it somehow meant to be, like a destiny kind of thing?

Becca did hand me this heart.

And this is what's stamped on it?

Love Her

Interesting.

Should I follow the advice?

Should I love Becca tonight?

Will she let me?

The things I could do to her—with my lips, my tongue, my cock…

A heavy wind rips down the walkway, reminding me of just how damn cold it is out here.

Yet here I am, my mind muddled by a barrage of sex-filled thoughts.

So get back to the room and maybe you can start doing those things you're thinking about to the woman you care so much about.

"Right." I pocket the candy once more.

Before I leave, I make a few selections from the vending machines—potato chips and pretzels. I opt not to buy any chocolate bars, as I think we've had our fill of candy.

Sugar and carbs.

I laugh.

At this rate, Becca and I will be up all night.

"Though that may not be the only reason we're up all night," I murmur as I start back to the room, provisions in hand.

That's right—I've decided I'm making a move.

If Becca rejects me, so be it.

I have to try.

My feelings for her are just too strong.

When I reach the room, Becca is standing in the doorway, waiting for me.

"Aren't you cold?" I ask.

She doesn't have her jacket on.

But she looks anything but frigid.

Far from it.

There's heat in her eyes and a tilt to her hips that is equal parts provocative and inviting.

"Lars," she murmurs, the snow swirling around us. "I'm actually not cold at all."

"Okay," I lamely state, holding up the snack bags. "I. uh, got us some food."

Grabbing my arm, she groans, "Just get in here."

Once I'm inside, Becca closes the door, the soft snick of the lock turning the only sound breaking the silence.

But then I hear Becca breathe as she turns to me.

I drop the bags of snacks onto the little table by the door and kick off my boots.

When I start taking off my coat, she walks over to me.

"Do you need any help?" she asks.

There's so much I want to say, a hundred things I long to ask.

But what do I do?

I just shake my head. "No, I'm good."

Becca touches my arm. "Lars…"

I'm supposed to be the one making the move, but she's beating me to it.

Quietly, I ask, "What happened while I was away?"

"This," she replies, holding out her hand, palm side up.

I look down to see one of those tiny candy hearts in the center of her palm.

I read what it says: *You're His.*

Raising my eyes to meet hers, I ask, "Is it true?"

Releasing a stuttered breath, Becca whispers, "Yes, it is."

I am not expecting that.

But I like it.

My heart starts beating like crazy and my soul soars.

This is what I want.

I have for a while.

Since the night in the theatre, since earlier today, for a long time now, I never wanted to be "just friends." I've wanted Becca from the beginning.

And now I know she wants me too, in the same way.

To be sure, though, I ask, "What about us just being friends? You told me you were scared of taking things any further. You wanted to protect your heart."

"That's true." Becca reaches out, caressing the light stubble on my cheek. "I was scared, Lars, and I still am. But it's not a choice I can make, not anymore. I can't keep denying what's really in my heart. Besides, I think I see now that maybe love is about being a little scared."

I cock my head, leaning into her touch. "What are you afraid of? What's been scaring you this whole time? I know it's not me personally. Is it just the thought of getting hurt?"

She blows out a breath, dropping her hand to her side.

I immediately feel the loss.

Sighing, she says, "I'm scared of the unknown, and of things not working out. There's more too, some fears I can't define. I'm afraid of just so much."

I reach over to where my jacket is hanging on the back of a chair and retrieve the candy heart from my pocket.

Placing it in her hand, I say, "Look, I can't promise you everything will always be easy. I think anything worthwhile never is. But let's give this a try. Just… let me…"

"Let you what, Lars?"

"Read my heart," I say, meaning so much more than the heart I just handed to her.

But it's the candy that she's staring down at now.

"Love her," she murmurs, reading the words out loud. Blinking up at me wide-eyed, she asks, "Do you?"

"Yes, Becca, I do. Somewhere along the line, I've fallen completely in love with you. It's not just what's written on the candy that's true." I tap my chest. "It's what's in here."

"Oh, Lars…"

There are tears in her eyes as I whisper, "Will you let me, then?"

"Let you what?"

"Isn't it obvious?" I laugh. "Let me love you."

Chapter
TWENTY-ONE

Will I Let Him Love Me?
Becca

*L*ars asks if I'll let him love me.

Will I?

Can I?

Do I?

If I'm honest with myself, this is everything I've ever wanted.

Lars is everything I've ever wanted.

I've known it for a while, a long while.

Am I done denying it?

I sigh as he waits for my answer.

Lars is a good man, and he's beautiful to look at. He's also kind and generous. But he's my friend first and foremost. There's always been this major attraction with us, an amazing chemistry brewing just beneath the surface.

Do I now let it boil over?

Do I have a choice?

"No," I say at last.

His face falls. "No?"

"Oh my God." I rush into his arms, leaning my cheek to his chest as I murmur, "I didn't mean 'no' to what you're asking."

He urges me back a few inches so he can see my face. "What are you saying exactly, then? I want us to be completely clear."

I nod. "I agree. I do too. So I'm saying yes, I want you to love me. Do you want to know why?"

"Yes," he says. "I'd like to know everything you're thinking."

I snicker. "Well, I can't tell you everything, but I can tell you this—I love you."

That sure leaves him speechless.

When he recovers from the shock, he asks incredulously, "You do?"

"Yes." I start backing him toward the bed, and he puts up no resistance. "And I'm about to show you just how much," I add silkily, promise in my tone.

The backs of his knees hit the edge of the heart-shaped mattress, and all I have to do is give a little push and Lars falls back onto the bed.

I crawl up his body, warning, "You're at my mercy now."

"Fuck yeah," he grinds out. "There's no place I'd rather be."

"Good. Same here."

I unbuckle his belt and start to get to work on his jeans, but then I realize we need to have a quick conversation about birth control and all that other fun stuff.

After we do, Lars says, "So we're both clean and you're already on the pill for other reasons."

"Yes," I affirm. "Now enough talking…"

I grab him again as I unbutton and unzip his jeans, tugging the denim material away.

Mmm, yes!

Once I have his jeans shimmied down his hips—with his help, of course—I place my hand over his boxer briefs to fully feel his massive erection.

When I give a little squeeze, Lars says roughly, "Damn it, woman. You better do more than that."

"Oh, I plan to." Coyly, I raise a brow. "Do you know how much I want this?"

"Tell me," he demands.

"A lot." I reach inside and grasp his full length. "So much I can't even find the words."

As I begin stroking, Lars rasps, "It's yours, Becca. *I'm* yours."

Gah!

I just want to jump him.

But I also want to remember every second of what's about to occur.

"I don't want to rush this," I share as I lift his long-sleeved tee, exposing the most sculpted, ripped abs I think I've ever seen. "I need to savor every inch of you."

"You took the words right out of my mouth," he replies, chuckling. "But it's going to be *me* savoring *you*."

"How about we both do a lot of savoring?" I suggest as I stretch out across his hard body.

"That works for me," he murmurs, his hand winding into my hair. "We should get started right away. No more talking, yeah?"

I nod. "Yes, no more talking."

There isn't much from there. We're too busy removing and tossing aside clothes, kissing each newly exposed bit of skin, sometimes licking, sometimes nipping, and sometimes tasting.

But always, always savoring.

Chapter
TWENTY-TWO

At Last

Lars

With every touch of her skin, every taste of her body, you'd think I'd be sated.

But no, I can't get enough of Becca.

"I want you so badly," I tell her.

We're bare, my body pressed to hers. She's coming apart from the things I just did to her with my mouth.

"So take me," she whispers, her voice thick with lust as she arches her back. "I'm going to die if you don't, Lars. I swear that I will."

I think she believes that.

Maybe I do too.

"You're still shaking," I note, caressing her cheek.

"That's because I'm ready for you. I have been for a while. I am *so* ready."

The tip of my cock is right where it needs to be, nudging at her warm folds.

I press in a little and she accepts me, gasping out my name.

She then begs for more.

I need no more invitation than that.

I have only so much strength to drag this out.

So I finally plunge into her warmth.

And she… is… perfection.

Becca cries out in pleasure, gripping me with her arms and with her pussy.

"More," she groans.

I give her even more.

I give her *all* of me.

I don't mean just my body.

I give her my heart.

But wait, she already has that.

"Lars, Lars, Lars," she chants in rhythm with my thrusting.

Fuck, I'm about to explode.

I have to slow things down.

I don't want this to end, not yet.

Cupping one of her breasts, I kiss along her silky, smooth neck.

I really do want to love her slowly, with all the caring and devotion I feel.

Has it ever been this good with anyone else?

Never.

This is true love.

This is life.

I whisper sweet nothings in Becca's ear as she moves with me. It's just her and I on this snowy night, loving each other on a heart-shaped bed in a love-themed motel room.

I almost start to laugh, but I can only smile.

I realize finding this place, the unexpected change in the weather, it's all been destined.

We are destined.

"I want to stay inside you forever," I admit.

It's the truth.

"I wish you could," Becca replies.

A shift of my hips and I hit a new spot that brings her to climax.

I follow shortly thereafter.

Sadly, I can't stay inside her forever.

But we still have the rest of the night.

I plan to have Becca in as many ways and positions as we can think of.

Turns out, that is quite a lot.

Chapter
TWENTY-THREE

Yes, I Freaking Love Snow
Becca

I've hated snow pretty much my entire life. But right now, on this night, I love the freaking white stuff.

Why the change?

Because it's this snow that doesn't seem to want to let up that's allowing us to create our own snowed-in love nest.

So yes, I now love snow.

I giggle as I stretch and think about how this motel sure has lived up to its name. I bet this heart-shaped bed hasn't seen this much action in ages. I mean, sure, no doubt a lot of people have loved in, and on, the silky pink sheets prior to Lars and me.

But I doubt many, if any, have kept pace with us.

"I think we're breaking records," I say to Lars, gasping as I feel him pushing into me from behind.

I don't know how many times we've had each other the past several hours, but it's been a lot.

Still, it's never enough.

"We're making up for lost time," he rasps in my ear.

"That we are," I agree, pressing my ass back against him so he can slide in all the way.

I moan, lost once more in an ecstasy I didn't know possible.

There's no more talking, only moving, pleasure, and joy.

Though Lars and I are insatiable, we do manage to get in *some* sleep in between our sessions of love.

Still, time is irrelevant.

It's just us, breaking barriers, becoming one.

As with all good things, though, our time of giving in to each other and caving to the feelings that have grown since that fateful day in the theatre comes to an end.

The light streaming in through a gap in the curtains on the lone window facing the front of the motel wakes me up early in the morning.

"Ugh, it's so bright in here," I murmur sleepily, covering my eyes with my hand.

My griping and subsequent huffing wake up Lars.

Stretching, he replies drowsily, "Hold on. I can fix it."

"Mmm…" I nuzzle in closer to him. "Thank you. You really are the best."

Chuckling, he says, "If you keep pressing up against me like that, I may just stay in bed."

Forgetting about the morning light for now, I murmur, "On second thought, I think you should do exactly that. Stay, love me some more."

He does.

Yeah, it takes another good thirty minutes before the curtains are tightly drawn, blocking out the light.

When Lars returns to the bed, he says, "It looks like it quit snowing."

"Is there a lot out there?" I ask.

"Tons."

Leaning into the crook of his arm, I want to know, "So what happens now?"

He looks worried. "Are you regretting what happened, Becca?"

Twisting to peer up at him, I shake my head. "No. I have no regrets at all. But things have changed. We can't deny that. It already feels different."

"Things have changed," he agrees as he leans down to kiss my forehead.

"Mmmm..."

As he settles back, he says, "They're different in the very best way, though."

"I think so too," I agree.

Chuckling, Lars clears his throat.

So I ask, "What?"

"Well, this is going to sound corny and like we're in junior high, but, Becca Nadeau, will you be my girlfriend?"

I laugh as I turn to him, hitching a leg over his hips. "It does sound like we're in seventh grade. But I know what you're asking."

He raises a brow. "So what's your answer, Potential Junior High Girlfriend?"

I laugh. "Yes, I want to be your girlfriend, but not just some junior high version. I want to be your grown-up girlfriend." I press against him seductively. "That way we can enjoy all the benefits that come with that."

Grabbing my ass, he says, "Damn, you're not kidding."

I grow serious then, though, when I say to Lars, "It wasn't just lust making me say the things I said to you last night. I have truly grown to love you."

He looks so damn happy hearing that, and tells me, "I feel the same way, Becca. I love you too."

I let out a little laugh, and he asks, "Hey, what's so funny about that?"

"It's not you professing your love that's making me laugh," I assure him. "I was just thinking how excited Jodi is going to be when she learns of this change in our relationship."

He cocks a brow. "You think so? Why's that?"

Grinning, I say, "Okay, let's review. First, she wants me happy, right?"

"Yes." Readjusting our bodies and propping up on an elbow, Lars asks, "And I make you happy?"

"Immensely." I touch his stubbled cheek. "But I think you already know that."

"I still like hearing it," he says. "Any other reasons Jodi's going to be thrilled we're a couple?"

"Yes." I nod excitedly. "She's going to see you made me believe again. And that is a very good thing."

Looking into my eyes, Lars asks, "What did I make you believe again, Becca?"

I blow out a breath, and tell him the truth, "You made me believe in love again. I told you once that I didn't believe in it any longer. I thought the fairy tale wasn't meant for me."

"But now you know it is," he says softly, cupping my chin so that I have to look up at him.

I nod, and he promises, "That is why, from this moment forward, my beautiful Becca, I am going to do everything in my power to make all of your dreams come true."

Chapter
TWENTY-FOUR

Looking to the Future with a Smile

Lars

I tell Becca I plan to make all of her dreams come true.

I do, even if it means I'll be busting my ass trying.

She deserves to be treated like a queen.

My queen.

"Lars," Becca says, tears welling in her eyes, "I want so badly to say how I feel right now."

"And how is that?" I ask.

"Elated. So freaking elated."

"Good." I snuggle her into my arms. "Then I'm going to keep doing whatever it takes to keep your heart filled with this kind of joy."

"Lars..." she begins, but a yawn escapes her.

Chuckling, I say, "Sleep, my love. Get some rest. We'll talk more about all of this good stuff later."

Shit, I'm dead tired too.

So we fall asleep then, contented and in love.

I wake up first.

A few hours have passed, and since we have to check out soon, I shower and dress.

Afterward, I figure I should head out and grab some breakfast for us. My woman can't live on love alone, and the snacks and candy have pretty much run out.

Since Becca is still asleep, I write her a quick note on a Post-it pad I find on the table by the door.

> Be right back, Becs.
>   Off to find us some food, something more than candy and snacks.
> Love you.
> Lars

Okay, I need to brush up on my romantic-note-writing skills, but it's the thought that counts.

Once I'm outside, I quickly discover there's more that needs brushing—like literally. My SUV is covered in a mountain of snow.

"Good thing I keep a snow brush in the back," I mutter out loud into the crisp cold and silence.

After grabbing the brush, I get to work.

A good while later—hey, there was a massive amount of that white crap that needed to be cleared—I'm traveling down the road in search of a fast food restaurant.

"Ah," I murmur when I catch sight of the golden arches. "I knew there'd be one of those."

I go through the drive-thru, returning to the motel with two different hot breakfast sandwiches, hash browns, and two orange juices.

Once I'm back, I find Becca is up and about. She's already showered and dressed too.

"Someone's ready to roll," I say.

She shrugs. "I know we have to leave soon."

She's seated on the bed, brushing out her damp honey-blonde hair, looking kind of sad.

"Yeah," I sigh resignedly as I set the drink holder with the two juices down on the table. "We probably should check out and get going. But first, let's eat." I hold up the bag. "My quest was successful, and though it's not the most nutritious food in the land, it is nice and warm."

Becca smiles as she stands.

I hand her the bag of fast food.

As she rummages through it, she says, "I actually am freaking starving."

"Guess we worked up an appetite, huh?"

She stops her digging long enough to smile over at me. "We sure did."

I start taking off my coat. "Choose whichever sandwich you like. I'll eat either one. I got hash browns too."

"Mmm, sounds good."

Becca opts for a sausage muffin sandwich and a hash brown.

"This looks so good," she says.

My stomach starts growling when I smell the food, reminding me that I am beyond famished.

Motioning to the bag, I say, "Hey, pass that bag over here."

"You got it."

Once I have my sandwich and hash brown, Becca and I set up an eating space on the table by the door.

When I fully open the curtains, her eyes widen. "Holy crap! That's a lot of snow."

"I told you there was a ton." I jerk my chin to the window, where my SUV is parked just outside. "You should've seen how long it took me to dig out the Nav."

Becca laughs between bites of her sandwich. "I bet it took a while. Good thing you had a snow brush. I noticed it in the back yesterday but never dreamed we'd need it."

"Right?" I take a sip of my juice. "Still, it barely did the job. I was about to go ask the motel lady if she had a broom."

Becca smiles. "That would've been a sight."

I just shake my head.

We finish our breakfast, straighten up the room a little, and then hit the road.

Becca was right—things do feel different now.

But I was right too—they're different in a really good way.

I can't believe how much has changed in such a short amount of time. Becca and I are no longer "just friends." We're lovers and officially a couple.

Who would have ever dreamed this trip could change so much?

I had no clue.

I'm glad it turned out this way. I was tiring of keeping my true feelings bottled up. I've wanted to date Becca from the beginning. She intrigued me from the moment she walked back to that last row in the theatre and sat down a few seats away.

I've been enthralled ever since.

When she catches me smiling, she asks, "What are you thinking about, Lars?"

Glancing over at her, I say, "I'm thinking about you… me… us."

Reaching over the console, she takes my hand. "This all feels so incredibly right, doesn't it?"

"It sure does, Becca." I release a breath. "It sure does."

Chapter
TWENTY-FIVE

Making Dreams Come True
Becca

When Lars and I return to Columbus, life is better than ever. Nothing changes in terms of our expressed love and upgraded relationship status from our time up at The Love Nest. I initially worried that perhaps reality would creep in and alter our perspective. But it hasn't. If anything, our relationship has grown stronger every day. Lars and I spend so much time together and get along beautifully.

One afternoon while Jodi and I are at our shop, catching up on work while seated at our desks, I notice her peering over at me.

She's smiling like crazy.

"What's up?" I ask. "Are you losing it or something?"

"Ha." She snorts. "I'm fine. If anyone is losing it, it's you."

Perplexed, I ask, "Wait. How do you mean?"

"You are clearly, completely lost in love with Lars."

"I can't argue that," I admit. "Guilty as charged."

My confirmation has Jodi practically bouncing in her chair.

"Yes!" She pumps her fist in the air. "You've finally found the love you deserve. I am so freaking happy for you, Becs. That's why I've been smiling over at you. Ooh, and I must tell you, Caleb is freaking thrilled for you guys too."

I laugh. "I knew you'd be happy. I told Lars as much. You and Caleb called it. You two always thought we'd be a good match. That's why you set us up on that double date in the first place."

"True. But we had no clue you'd already met Lars. And—" She grins over at me mischievously. "—you'd totally made out with him."

Coyly, I remark, "And now we've done sooo much more than that."

"Ooh, speaking of which…" Jodi rubs her hands together evilly. "We haven't had much time to talk. And I need details! You've been keeping the goods all to yourself. So tell me. How is that hot hunk of man in the sack?"

My eyes widen. "You are so bad. Hot hunk of a man, huh? Don't worry, I won't tell Caleb you just called his friend and teammate that. But for the record, Lars is ahhhh-mazing in bed. He has a lot of, uh, stamina, shall we say. I swear the man can go all night."

Smiling like she's in on the secret, Jodi says, "I know, right? Football players do seem to have a lot of endurance… and skill."

I shrug. "Maybe. But I think we just got good ones."

"Yeah," she concedes, "you're probably right. Dumbo, the worst quarterback in the world, was a real loser. I bet he sucked in bed."

Dumbo, aka Dan, was once the Comets' quarterback. For a multitude of reasons, he's long gone from Columbus. Good thing too, as he was not only a terrible QB but an even more awful person.

"Ugh, enough about him," I say. "But I do have a question."

"Yes?"

"Regarding the quarterback situation, what's going on with the search for a new one? Lars mentioned something about an interest in some guy named Graham Tettersaw. Has Caleb heard anything about him?"

Shaking her head, Jodi says, "Not a whole lot, no. The team seems to be keeping things on the down low for now. Still, Caleb heard a rumor that the Comets started talking to Tettersaw's agent. He heard if all goes well, Graham may be coming into town for mini-camp next month."

"Wow," I marvel. "I can't believe it's almost May."

"Yeah, our guys are about to get real busy, real soon."

"That makes me a little sad," I admit. "I kind of like having Lars all to myself."

Jodi reminds me that our wedding planning business is also picking up, so we'll be busy too.

"We're entering prime wedding season now," she states with a flourish of the pen she just picked up.

"True," I agree.

Though I'm thrilled I'll have many things to occupy my time, I'm sad there's about to be a big change in my life with Lars. We spend *so* much time together. I'm always at his place or he's at mine, and when we're not hanging out, we're running around town having fun.

Lars really has stuck by what he told me at The Love Nest—he's been trying really hard to make all of my dreams come true.

I do the same for him too.

But now I'm afraid things will change and our balance will be upset.

Later that night, I share my fears with Lars.

We're in his bed, which, though it's not heart-shaped, has seen just as much action lately as The Love Nest bed.

No, wait, it's seen much more, the latest session having wrapped up only five minutes ago.

In fact, I'm still feeling warm and fuzzy from a slew of orgasms as I nuzzle into Lars's warm, hard, bare body.

Sighing, I say, "I'm scared things are going to change, especially when you get busy."

Holding onto me tightly, he assures, "Becca, nothing is going to change, at least not in any kind of negative way. I'll just be doing more than working out at the gym all the time once mini-camp gets underway."

"I know, I know." I shake my head. "You're right. I feel like this shouldn't bother me so much. You have to get back to your job, right?"

"I do."

Sighing, I concede, "Maybe it's the fear of the unknown that has me all weirded out. I don't know, but something is nagging at me. I just can't put my finger on it."

Kissing the top of my head, Lars says, "Don't worry so much, okay? Change can be scary, yes. But I think it's actually going to be more fun once I get busier."

"Yeah, how so?"

"You can come to some of my practices and watch me do my thing in person. That'll be cool, right?"

"I would like that." Raising my head, I peer up into his deep brown eyes. "I really would."

It's true that I'm super excited to see my man in action on the field in person. I've watched so much game footage, witnessing his amazing talent, but there's no substitute for watching him in real life.

I'm looking forward to the games too, the ones that count.

Too bad the season is so far away.

Maybe that's what's scaring me?

There's so much time between now and then, where so many things could happen.

Ugh, that overwhelming feeling of foreboding rushes back over me, like a wave of despair.

I feel like there really is something hanging over our happiness, waiting to cut it short.

I sense it deep in my soul.

And that's what has me really worried.

No matter how irrational, and despite all of Jodi's and Lars's reassurances, I have a sense of dread that my world is about to be turned upside down.

I just don't know how, why, or when.

Chapter
TWENTY-SIX

Mini-Camp Surprise

Lars

I'm running my route down the practice field, turning when and where I'm supposed to.

Yep, there's the ball.

It's a perfect pass that floats right into my hands.

This is how it's supposed to work.

Cradling the football securely, I run into the end zone.

Touchdown!

I'm so fast that nobody was on my ass. I mean, a few guys on defense have now caught up to me, but they're too late.

That pass, though—perfection.

That's all I can think about right now, even as I celebrate with a few of my teammates on our offensive squad.

Mini-camp is underway, and today is practice scrimmage number four. Yesterday Becca was here, watching me make my moves. I was kicking ass then too. I have to give a lot of credit to this Graham Tettersaw guy. We work well together. I'm glad the Comets brought him in for a tryout to fill the vacant starting quarterback position.

He's solid.

I like him.

I hope the team hires him.

We need a quality QB like Tettersaw.

I guess we'll see where things land, as I have no say in the decision. That's why I'm focused on simply being the best receiver I can be.

There's another wide receiver on the team—Zane Tinsbury. He's been giving me some stiff competition for that number one spot. I may have been the star yesterday and today, but he's been shining like a motherfucker, having had some great receptions earlier this week.

Today, though, it's all me.

After the scrimmage ends, and once we're on our way to the locker room, Zane catches up to me to give me props for my performance on the field.

"Good scrimmage, man," he says. "You looked fast and on the ball out there."

"Thanks." I take off my helmet and rake my fingers through my sweat-damp hair. "I can't take all the credit, though. This quarterback prospect the Comets brought in, Graham, is really fucking good."

"He is, man," Zane agrees, nodding. "He is."

"I sure hope the Comets sign him."

We sit down on a bench and start taking off our gear when Zane replies, "Yeah, I do too. They may... or they may not."

"Why do you say that?" I ask.

He shrugs. "It's just that I've been hearing there are a lot of changes in store for the *whole* team, including a few key trades."

"Whoa, that's news to me." I swallow hard.

This could be good... or this could be bad.

One thing for sure, I don't want to be traded to another team. I like it here. Hell, I bought a house not all that long ago. That's why I stayed for the off-season, for fuck's sake.

But bigger than all that, what would a trade mean for me and

Becca?

Her life is here. She has her own business with Jodi, and it's successful. It's not like she'd give all that up for me.

I couldn't ask her to.

Running a hand down my face, I ask Zane, "Have you heard of anyone specifically that's on the trading block? Our wide receiver jobs aren't in danger, are they?"

He shakes his head. "Shit, man, I don't think so. I sure as fuck hope not. But I really don't know. My impression is pretty much any of us could be traded."

Fuck!

I rake my fingers through my hair, frustrated. "Man, I can't believe this is the first I'm hearing any of this."

"I assure you, it's not the last," Zane says. "There's chatter that the Comets are making these decisions soon too."

"Crap."

Once I'm undressed and in a towel, I seek out Caleb before I hit the showers. I need to ask if he's heard anything about this trade talk.

When I find him, I express my concerns, finishing with, "Is this news to you too?"

He tells me, "Yes, it is. I haven't heard anything about any trades."

Since he's clearly as out of the loop as I am, I fill him in on what else Zane had to say.

Caleb blows out a breath. "We had such a horrible inaugural season. I really wouldn't be surprised if this is all true."

"That's not exactly reassuring," I state sourly. "But unfortunately, I think you're right."

I finally hit the showers, feeling like crap.

Becca and I have plans tonight, like we do almost every night. We're going to have a nice, quiet dinner over at her house.

We'll probably hang out on her back porch afterward. The weather's been so nice lately; perfect for lazing around on the wooden Adirondack chairs she has out there.

Man, I love sipping iced tea with her and talking about whatever comes to mind.

We've been so happy lately; we get along beautifully.

I'm sure tonight will unfold in the same peaceful manner.

Everything is perfection.

Er, maybe not.

Now that there's trade talk hanging over my head, threatening our idyllic life, our happiness is in jeopardy.

Do I mention what I heard today to Becca?

Or should I keep it quiet for now?

What to do, what to do…

Fuck, I hate this.

Chapter
TWENTY-SEVEN

A Potential Disaster
Becca

After Lars and I eat dinner, we head out to the porch in the back of my house to chill for a while.

Since I live off the beaten path, down a long country road, I have only two neighbors. Neither is close. That means my back porch is private and perfect for enjoying evenings like the one tonight, with no one looking on.

I breathe it all in when we step outside. The spring air is warm, and the smell of blossoms permeates the air.

It's so relaxed out back, just like Lars and I are these days.

I can't believe I've found such true happiness.

Life is just so good.

And, bonus, I haven't felt uneasy lately like I did early on in our relationship. I think peace has finally found me. I'm no longer worried something will tear us apart.

Before Lars and I sit down on the Adirondack chairs, I move mine a little closer to his. They're already side by side, but I can never be too close to my wonderful man.

I sigh as I take a seat, content with how our relationship is progressing. I guess my earlier concerns were for nothing.

There's a small table on the other side of my chair, and I set my tall glass of iced tea there. Lars has a table on his side as well and does the same, letting out a long sigh.

Wait, that's not a contented exhale of air.

No, he sounds stressed.

"Did you have a rough day?" I ask carefully. "You didn't mention much about practice at dinner. Did it not go well this afternoon?"

I did most of the talking while we ate supper, filling Lars in on a couple of upcoming weddings Jodi and I are consulting on. He listened attentively, but now I'm wondering if his mind was actually somewhere else.

Hmmm…

"Practice was fine today," he replies, picking up his iced tea and taking a quick sip. After he sets the glass back down, he adds, "Just like yesterday when you were there, I was feeling it out on the field."

"That's great," I say. "Sounds like you're still on fire."

Hedging, he says, "Yeah, I guess so. I got in a few more good reps when we scrimmaged. I even ran in some touchdowns."

"Wow, that's fantastic." I'm excited to hear practice went well, and I twist in my chair so I can face Lars more fully. "So why don't you sound more thrilled? More importantly, why are you keeping all this to yourself?"

"I'm not," he counters. "I'm telling you now."

"Yeah, but you should've told me all this good news sooner."

Lars shakes his head humbly. "Nah. It wasn't just me out there making the good plays. I can't take all the credit. Graham threw some amazing passes."

I nod. "Yeah, he did look really good yesterday."

"He was the same today," Lars replies.

Huh.

Even though he's telling me all these positive things, Lars seems bothered by something.

So I press. "Did something bad happen that you're leaving out? You don't sound all that enthused about today's practice."

"Ah, hell…" He runs his hand down his chiseled face, and I get the feeling I'm about to find out what's really going on.

Sure enough, he says, "I wasn't going to say anything to cause you any unnecessary worry. But I have to be honest."

"Uh oh." I cringe. "Honest about what?"

"I heard something today that has me worried."

"What did you hear?"

Leaning back in his chair, Lars peers up at the planked porch ceiling, mouth set in a grim line.

"Okay, this can't be good."

"No, it's not. I was talking with one of the other wide receivers, Zane, and he told me he heard the Comets are planning to make some key trades."

That sense of dread I had in the past returns with a vengeance.

Getting straight to the point, I ask, "They wouldn't trade *you*, though, would they?"

Lars shrugs, which is not reassuring at all. "I don't know, Becca. I kind of get the feeling from what Zane said that no one is safe."

I throw my hands up in the air. "But you're their best wide receiver. You're better than Zane. Maybe he should be the one worrying?"

Lars shrugs. "Maybe, but I have the bigger contract." He glances over at me. "That makes me a liability of sorts, especially when trading me could free up money to sign a good quarterback. One like Graham."

I feel dizzy. "B-b-but then the Comets would be down a receiver."

"Not if they traded for one who's cheaper than me."

"I can't sit." I jump up. "I'm about to go crazy here." Frustrated, I start pacing the length of the porch. Back and forth, back and forth, until I cry out, "Lars, they can't do this!"

Remaining seated and looking resigned, he says, "Ah, but they can, sweetheart. It's their team. We're merely pieces on their chessboard."

"It's not right," I insist, sniffling as I lean my black leggings-clad butt against the wooden railing, the night air feeling far colder than it did ten minutes ago.

Lars gets up and comes over to me.

Encircling me in his strong, comforting arms, he says, "Let's just see what happens, okay? All of this worrying could be for nothing."

"I hope you're right," I mumble into his shoulder. "God, I hope you're right."

And then I start to cry.

Chapter
TWENTY-EIGHT

A Devastating Blow
Lars

I hold Becca in my arms until she calms down.

When she leans back, sniffling, I ask her, "Do you want to go inside?"

"Yes." She nods. "I do."

Her lips then find mine.

I kiss her back desperately with a sudden unquenched need.

It's a new urgency we clearly both feel, a sense that this could all end.

Or at least be derailed from the track we've been on.

It's been such a great track too, a damn good ride.

I don't want our relationship to change in any way, shape, or form.

I see a future with Becca, one I never imagined with any other woman.

Only with her.

That's why I need to lose myself inside of her as soon as possible.

Thank God she's just as needy.

With both of us desperate, we don't even make it up the stairs. Bedroom be damned; the floor serves our needs.

Good thing this part of her house is covered in plush carpeting.

Clothes are but a hindrance and they're quickly removed.

I can finally have her.

And I do.

Becca cries out when I first pump into her, but she's soon begging, "Harder, Lars, harder."

I comply, as I need it like this too.

Frenzied, she meets my every thrust, sometimes even more forcefully than how hard I'm plunging into her.

Her warmth comforts me.

This isn't about getting off, not for either of us. This is a union of two people who have fallen deeply in love and now feel threatened with cataclysmic change.

This is an escape, a diversion we both crave.

"You are everything to me, Becca," I murmur as I lift one of her legs so I can plunge into her more deeply.

Before I can, she stops me with a hand to my chest. "You are everything to me too, Lars," she says. "That's why whatever happens, we'll figure this out. We *will* make it through whatever comes our way."

"Yes, we will. But"—I lift her leg higher—"enough talking for now."

That gets her to smile.

And then she's moaning and coming apart—with me, together, as one.

After we clean up, we make our way over to the sofa, where we both fall asleep, with Becca sprawled out on top me.

At some point, I rouse and wake her. "We should go up to bed."

"Yes." She nods sleepily.

Slowly, we head to her bedroom.

It's Friday night, so there's no practice tomorrow. I'm looking forward to sleeping in and spending all morning with Becca. Every minute feels precious now. Maybe I'll even surprise her and make us breakfast.

I've learned to make healthy versions of those muffin sandwiches we indulged in when we were up in New York. They're amazing too. I use plant-based sausage, whole wheat muffins, fresh eggs from a local farm, and low-fat cheese.

Becca loves them.

That is my last thought before I doze off.

I sleep fitfully, though, tossing and turning.

Despite advising her not to worry about a trade, I'm extremely concerned.

I do not want to go anywhere.

My life is here.

My life is Becca.

Snuggling into this woman I've fallen so hard for, I finally find the peace to rest.

But I wake up early.

Since Becca is still sleeping, I'm careful not to wake her.

After I'm up and dressed in gray sweats, I head downstairs to get on with making that breakfast I was thinking about before I nodded off.

In the kitchen, I poach eggs and fry up the veggie sausages.

I guess the breakfast aromas wake up Becca, as she shows up in the doorway, yawning, her hair an adorable mess.

I can't help but smile as I say, "Hey, sleepyhead. Hope you're hungry."

She looks fucking adorable in the hot pink sleep shorts and tee she must've slipped on after getting up.

Nodding sleepily, she assures me she is indeed hungry.

I catch her licking her lips, her eyes trailing down my bare chest to my low-slung sweatpants.

Hell, I know that look.

It takes everything in me not to walk over, say to hell with breakfast, and peel those cute pink sleep clothes right the hell off her hot body.

In fact, I think I might...

But then my cell phone rings.

"Who in the hell could that be?" I gripe as I reach for the damn thing over on the counter. "It's Saturday morning."

Becca shrugs. "I don't know. You better get it, though. It could be important."

I know she and I are both thinking the same thing—it may be about a trade.

I take a look at the screen and mutter, "Fuck."

"Who is it?" she asks as the phone continues to ring.

"It's my agent."

"Oh, hell," she breathes out, knowing full well this could be the call we've both been dreading. "Answer it, Lars."

"Okay." I place the call on speaker.

Becca deserves to hear whatever it is I'm about to.

When my agent starts talking, it's clear from the start that this is bad news. I can tell from his dour tone even as we exchange pleasantries.

And then he gets to why he's calling—the Dover Sharks, a football team in Delaware, are interested in me.

He says, "Lars, if the deal goes through, the Sharks would pick up your contract from the Comets. They may even add a year. All in return for one of their 'cheaper' wide receivers and a future first round draft pick."

"Crap, they must really like me."

"They do," he says.

"What if I don't want to go?"

Somberly, my agent explains, "It doesn't matter what you want or don't want. This is a decision that will be made by the Sharks and the

Comets. Not by you."

I place my free hand on the counter.

I need it for support.

I can hardly believe this is happening.

I listen to my agent as he tells me that though it looks probable, it's not a "done deal."

That gives me a glimmer of hope.

Becca must be feeling the same, as I hear her blow out a relieved breath.

"The Sharks would like to see you in action before making any solid decisions," my agent says. "You'll be flying out to Dover this upcoming week. I'll make all the arrangements online and get back to you."

"Yeah, that sounds just wonderful," I mutter sarcastically.

Once I wrap up with my agent, I place the phone back down on the counter with a *clunk*.

I'm afraid to look over at Becca.

I know what I'll see in her eyes—hurt, disappointment, disbelief, and a myriad of other emotions I can't even fathom at this point.

That's why I just stare at the granite countertop until my vision gets blurry.

It's only when Becca comes over and places her hand on my back that I realize I can't avoid the inevitable.

So I turn to her.

There are tears in her eyes, plus all the emotions I anticipated.

Neither of us says a word.

There's no need.

We both know our relationship has just been dealt a potentially devastating blow.

Chapter
TWENTY-NINE

Keep On Running
Becca

I was right to be scared.

I knew this relationship was too good to be true.

I should never have opened my heart.

I should've kept on running, like when I bolted from the theatre.

Somewhere deep inside, I knew it then—Lars and I are doomed.

Fate is freaking out to get me, I swear.

But it's not so easy to just take off.

I'm in it now.

I go to Lars, placing my hand on his bare back.

His skin is so warm and smooth to the touch.

It reminds me that he's here… but most likely not for long.

He turns to me.

He sees the tears in my eyes, the despair, the question of what do we do now.

At last, he shrugs.

He's as broken about this as I am.

Finally I whisper, "I tried to be strong and will them away. My tears, that is. I just couldn't do it."

As one lone traitorous tear escapes, trailing down my cheek, Lars brushes it away with his thumb.

"Me leaving is not a sure thing," he says. "You heard my agent. The Sharks are just 'interested' at this point."

"Yeah, right, just interested…" I trail off, laughing bitterly.

I am having none of this pep talk.

"Let's not sugarcoat it, Lars," I snap. "You're probably going to end up leaving Ohio for good."

Softly, he admits, "I can't lie. There is a strong chance that will happen."

"A better than strong chance," I counter. "You said it yourself—the Comets could save lots of money by unloading your contract. And the Sharks would finally have the great receiver they so badly want and need."

"Becca—"

I shake my head, holding up a hand. "Can we drop this subject? Please?"

"All right, sure. Do you want to eat breakfast still?"

"No."

My appetite is ruined, so Lars shuts down all the cooking.

After we place the sausage muffin sandwiches he made into plastic containers, we put them in the fridge.

"Do you want to go to the living room?" he asks.

"Sure."

I am numb.

Once we're seated on the sofa, Lars leans back and runs his hand down his face. "Becca, please, don't shut me out."

"I'm trying not to."

"But you are. I feel it. And we don't even know what's happening yet."

"That's true." I sigh. "I guess this is life, huh? Always throwing curveballs."

I feel a fresh round of tears coming on, and Lars, noticing, says, "Hey, let's focus on something else. Like our good times, okay?"

"How do you mean?" I ask, sniffling.

"I don't know. Let's do a little reminiscing. Thinking of all of our fun times always lifts my spirits when I'm feeling down."

Blinking over at him, I ask, "You think about us to feel better?"

Scooting closer, he places his hand on my knee. "I do, Becca. I reminisce about us a lot. And you know what?"

"What?"

"It works. Doing so makes me feel better every time."

"Okay"—I lean the other way from him so I can rest my back against the sofa arm and stretch my legs across his lap—"let's do it."

Chuckling and squeezing my calf, he says, "Okay, we'll start with this one, one of my faves. Do you remember our first night at the theatre?"

I laugh. "How could I ever forget?"

"Right?"

"So what about it?"

Raising a brow, he asks, "What did you really think of me at first?"

"Ah, that's an easy one. I thought you were super hot."

He looks at me doubtfully. "You could see all the way to the back of the theatre in that dim lighting?"

"Enough to know you were sexy, yes."

"Is that why you came back to sit in the last row with me?"

"Hell, yeah!"

"I kind of knew that," he replies smugly.

"Hey!" Sitting up, I playfully smack his arm.

Smirking, he tells me, "You weren't exactly subtle, Becs."

"Lars!" I reach over and shove his shoulder. "You're still so freaking arrogant."

Turning serious, he says, "Don't worry. The feeling was more than mutual." A smile creeps across his face. "Then you freaking kissed me out of the blue, and I was like 'Whoa, this is my kind of woman.'"

I snort. "I'm glad *you* felt that way. I came to my senses and realized I could be making out with a serial killer."

"Oh, Becca…" He rolls his eyes. "Is that why you ran off?"

Sheepishly, I reply, "Er, partly."

I don't want to admit it was also because I was afraid of what's happening now—I felt terrified that if I ever got him, this gorgeous man would leave me someday.

Lars peers over at me curiously.

He knows I'm thinking negative thoughts again.

Dazzling me with a fantastic smile that instantly cheers me up, he says, "I'm glad you came to your senses."

I harrumph. "As I recall, I only agreed to friendship in the beginning."

"Ugh." He runs both hands down his face. "That was so hard. It was like you were running again, just like that night at the theatre. But this time, you were running from your emotions."

"Very perceptive," I muse.

"It does seem to be your go-to response, babe."

"It always has been," I quietly admit. "I'm a runner at heart."

Moving my legs aside, he rises up till he's hovering over me.

In a husky voice, he says, "Then I'm glad I caught you."

Lifting, so our lips can touch, I murmur, "I am too."

I feel like I must kiss Lars right now. But we're interrupted when his stupid phone starts ringing again.

"Good God, I thought you left that damn thing in the kitchen," I lament.

"I should have," he grumps.

Sitting up, he answers the call, placing the phone on speaker once more so I can hear.

It's his annoying agent again, no surprise there, calling with Lars's flight info.

"You leave tomorrow for Dover at six a.m.," he says.

Frowning, Lars says, "Fuck, that's early. Plus, tomorrow is Sunday."

"Sorry, but the Sharks need you there as soon as possible. And workouts are going on all this week and next, including Sundays. There's one tomorrow at noon, and they expect you to be there."

Lars sighs. "All right, okay. How many days do they want me to stay?"

"Days?" His agent guffaws. "Get ready to hunker down in Dover for the next two weeks, bro."

Ugh, this sucks already.

Lars talks to his agent for the next few minutes, but I tune them out.

When he finally gets off the phone, I say, "So you leave tomorrow and you'll be gone for two weeks, huh?"

"Yes. So"—he raises a brow and tugs at the hem of my shorts—"I think this means we need to make the most of our time together. Starting right now..."

I can't argue with that.

Chapter THIRTY

Swimming with Sharks
Lars

This night of loving Becca is all I have. So you bet your ass I make the most of it, bringing her to climax again and again.

I leave her house long before dawn so I can race home, pack a bag, and make it to the airport in time for my early flight.

She cried before I left.

Shit, I almost did too.

I told her again that it'll all work out.

Will it?

I don't know.

After I land in Dover, I meet with a driver and limo waiting to take me to the hotel I'll be staying in.

But I only have time to drop off my bag.

The team already has checked me in.

I'm told via text that there will be a rental car waiting for me at the training facility. I can drive it back to the hotel after practice.

These Sharks don't mess around. They run this shit like a well-oiled machine.

I'm driven from the hotel to the training facility in the limo. It's state-of-the-art and there's already a stall in the locker room set up for me.

I'm a few minutes late getting out on the field, having no real time to get acquainted with the players.

Once I'm out there, things start right away.

These Sharks are pretty regimented. This is not like the Comets' laid-back mini-camp.

The coach, an old man with white hair and brown leathery skin, tells me, "I want you one-on-one with the quarterback. You'll be running these routes." He hands me several pieces of paper outlining the plays. "With just the two of you, I can better assess your chemistry."

"Okay." I nod as I look over the plays.

It's an interesting approach, this jump-right-in tactic, but I can roll with it. Even though I don't want to leave Columbus, I'm committed to doing my best during my time in Dover.

That's just me.

I'm a natural competitor.

The Sharks' quarterback is friendly enough. His name is Mike. I've met him before, since we played the Sharks during our regular season.

"Hey, man," he says, shaking my hand. "Good to see you again. Welcome to our camp."

"Thanks," I reply.

We review the plays together, and then get started.

It's pretty basic stuff—a lot of me running down the field in various patterns, catching passes.

Their quarterback has a good arm, but I like Graham better. I'd rather play with him than this guy.

That is, if the Comets pick up Graham Tettersaw.

And keep me.

All their decisions seem to be on hold lately.

That sucks, because the last thing Becca and I need is for me to be gone for two weeks only to return to find out our lives are still up in the air.

Unfortunately, I have a feeling that's the way it will play out.

After I run the final route Coach asks to see—a simple down-and-out pattern—Mike asks if I'd like to go out with the guys tonight.

I have nothing else to do, and I sure as hell don't relish the idea of sitting alone in my hotel room all evening, so I say, "Sure."

"Great. There's a cool bar and grill where we hang a lot," Mike tells me. "We'll be heading over there later for a few cold beers."

"Where is this place?" I ask. "I have a rental car with GPS. So I can drive myself."

"Actually," he says, "I'll just pick you up at the hotel where you're staying. It'll be easier, as I'm not planning on drinking tonight. I'm taking cold medicine, so no booze for me. Plus, this way you can have a drink or two with the guys and not worry about having to drive."

"What about the guys, though?" I ask.

"They're renting a shuttle," he tells me. "That's an option too."

Since I'd rather ride with Mike than a bunch of guys I don't know at all, I say, "I'll go with you."

"Perfect." He nods. "Want to meet in the hotel lobby around seven?"

"Sure."

Practice continues a short while longer, and then I hit the showers. My rental car is in the players' parking lot just as I was informed it would be. I drive it to the hotel.

It's almost five by the time I'm back up in my room.

I remember Becca mentioning that she had an appointment with a client around this time, so I decide not to call.

But I do send her a text letting her know I'm going out with the boys at seven. I say for her to call me as soon as she has a chance. I also let her know that even if I'm with the guys, I'll make time for her.

I always will.

Becca texts back pretty quickly with an assurance she'll call me later.

She adds, **Have fun. Gotta go for now. I'm with that new client, and she's really, uh, something. *insert sarcasm***

I laugh.

It's just as I thought—Becca is stuck with a pain-in-the-ass bride-to-be.

But this chick must really be "something," seeing as six o'clock rolls around, and then six thirty, and still there's no call or any further texts from Becca.

I think about sending her another quick message, but I don't want to bug her while she's working.

Resigned that I'll just talk to her later tonight, I slip the phone into my jeans pocket and head down to the lobby to meet with Mike.

Chapter
THIRTY-ONE

And So It Begins
Becca

*O*h my God, I am going to scream. Funny how some clients can be a dream… and others are a complete nightmare.

The one I'm dealing with today is a high-maintenance chick named Skye. She is, unfortunately, of the nightmare variety.

Skye must have at least thirty lists of requirements for her wedding, no joke. All are enumerated with things she'd like for me and Jodi to do for her and her upcoming nuptials.

I am going to kill my partner for not being here with me to deal with this crap!

It's my fault, though.

I agreed to meet with the Skye at five, outside of our normal business hours. I did it in the hopes of keeping my sad ass busy, as this is the first night Lars is away.

Jodi offered to stay, but I told her to go home to Caleb.

So, yeah, this is on me.

I said to her, "This way, one of us will have a good night."

She smiled over at me sadly, assuring me, "There are many good nights with Lars ahead of you, Becca."

"I hope you're right," I replied glumly.

I caught her looking away then, and that told me all I needed to know—there really is a chance Lars may be traded away.

Ugh!

My distressing reverie is cut short when my client blurts out, "By the way, I'd like for *all* of my guests to have not only favors but also a fresh floral arrangement of their own to take home."

"I advise against it," I reply. "You do realize it's going to cost quite a lot, right? Flowers can get real expensive, real fast."

"It doesn't matter." She sniffs haughtily. "My father is paying for everything."

"Still," I go on, "I'd rethink floral arrangements for *every* guest. Even favors are often left behind. There's a good chance flowers will be discarded on the tables. Then there's also the issue of fresh flowers not lasting very long."

I stop short of telling her it's a blatant waste of money, seeing as she is the client. I'm simply the consultant.

But it doesn't matter; Skye's mind is made up.

That much is clear when she insists on *all* the flowers. "I told you, money is no object," she states.

Sighing, I make a note to order two hundred and fifty *small* floral arrangements. I add another notation to be sure to notify the event facility to donate any leftover flowers to the nursing home down the street from them.

It makes me feel better knowing no flowers will be thrown away.

Grrr, I hate waste.

Skye continues to keep me busy from that point on. Our consultation lasts for almost three freaking hours.

The only good thing that comes out of it is I forget about Lars being away.

I'm quickly reminded, though, once I'm home.

My house is far too quiet.

That would be fine if I were preparing to go over to his place, or if he were coming to mine. I'd be making us dinner, or he'd arrive early and help.

But none of those things are happening tonight.

I check the time, noting how many hours I have to get through till I can go to sleep. Then I'll be one day closer to my man coming home.

Hmm, it's a few minutes after eight.

I have a while.

Lars said he'd be out with the guys, but he also mentioned for me to call anyway.

So I do.

Unfortunately, after several rings, I'm sent to voice mail.

Crap.

I think about leaving a short message for him to call back when he can.

But I decide not to.

I'll just try him again in a little while.

I should probably eat, as I'm starving. Skye the unruly client kept me from dinner.

I head to the kitchen and pull out a frozen dinner from the freezer. It's some sort of low-cal lasagna, but it'll do. I also—*score!*—find some leftover mixed green salad in the fridge.

"I'm all set," I murmur to myself as I poke holes in the plastic overlay to vent the lasagna before I place it in the microwave.

A short while later, while I'm seated at my small kitchen table, blowing on a bite of piping hot lasagna to cool it down, I hit Call again on my cell in the hopes of reaching Lars.

But once more, I'm sent to voice mail.

"Huh, that's weird."

I check the time.

It's nearing nine.

Didn't Lars say he was going out with the guys at seven?

Guess they're having a really good time, so good that he must not be checking his phone.

The ringer is probably turned off.

Ah, well.

I finish my lasagna and salad and decide not to dwell on it. Lars will call me once he's back in his hotel room.

I try to relax by washing the dishes by hand, and then hunkering down on the sofa in the living room.

I turn on the TV.

Only problem is I can't concentrate.

It's nine thirty, and I've still not heard a word from Lars.

I don't want to be a pest, but I go ahead and try him again.

I get his voice mail once more.

This time I leave a short message.

I also text to **Call me when you can**.

But he never does.

By eleven o'clock, as I'm heading to bed, there's still no communication from Lars.

I'm actually kind of worried.

This is not like him.

I sure hope nothing bad has happened.

Chapter
THIRTY-TWO

Bad Decisions

Lars

*H*oly hell!

When Mike mentioned a cool bar and grill where the guys like to hang, I envisioned a quiet, low-key establishment.

This place is anything but.

It's packed with people, and the music is blaring. For a Sunday night, this is wild.

The guys and I luck out and find a large round table in the bar area when a group of six—same as ours—leaves.

"I got the first round of shots for everyone," Mike announces once we're all seated. "Jamesons sound good?"

The guys all cheer, agreeing that Irish whiskey is a solid choice.

I join in the cheering, but wow, we haven't even ordered any beer yet.

That's rectified as soon as the waitress, looking completely frazzled with her messy auburn bun and pen behind her ear, comes over to take our orders.

Since no one has had dinner, we also all order food.

Oh, and the shots, of course, courtesy of Mike.

I'm happy to see he abstains like he told me he would—he asks for a Coke for himself—seeing as he's driving.

When the waitress returns with our beers and shots, I take the opportunity to check my phone to see if Becca has contacted me yet.

There's nothing from her.

I sigh.

It's seven thirty.

She must still be busy with the client.

Shaking my head and feeling bad for my poor girl, I set the phone, screen-down, on the table.

The waitress sets my beer right next to it, as well as the shot from Mike.

I nod and thank her.

Everyone takes their shot, and then we all start shooting the breeze.

I have to say the guys are really friendly. I find them welcoming, and I feel like I fit in. This is definitely a fun group.

Maybe playing here wouldn't be so bad?

If only I could talk Becca into coming to Dover with me. That is if they do indeed pick me up.

Yeah, right, that's never going to happen.

I mean, I could get traded to the Sharks, yeah. But Becca coming with me and leaving her whole life behind?

I just don't think we're there yet.

Nor could I ask her to give up everything she's worked so hard for.

I'm not that selfish.

Feeling cruddy about things and how they may turn out, I order another round of shots for everyone but Mike, making mine a double.

Mike, who is seated to my right, raises a brow. "Whoa, Samuels, you're going for it, huh?"

Shrugging, I reply, "What the hell. Practice doesn't start till noon tomorrow."

"That's true," he agrees.

"I'm sure I'll sleep it off by then."

"That's the spirit," one of the other men in the group chimes in when he overhears me.

Mike just shakes his head, chuckling.

Next round, everyone except for Mike orders a double shot.

Needless to say, we're all pretty buzzed by the time our dinners arrive.

We're louder and more boisterous too, at times even drowning out the blaring music.

That's quite a feat.

None of the other patrons seem to mind, though, as the whole damn bar is raucous.

Dinner flies by, plates are cleared, and someone buys me another shot of Irish whiskey.

I don't even think to check the time.

My phone is tucked under the red cloth napkin the waitress forgot to take.

I reach for it at one point to see if Becca has called, but I'm quickly distracted when the guy to my left and a couple of the others get up to mingle.

Mike stays at the table, as he's deep in conversation with a dude who's a safety on the team.

I watch as three of my potential teammates head over to talk to three women at the bar.

I look around the joint, observing that there sure are a lot of women in here.

That's probably why the guys like this bar so much.

The waitress comes by then, distracting me from my thoughts.

"Here you go," she says as she sets another beer down on the table.

"Whoa, hold up." I stop her before she leaves. Pointing to the bottle, I say, "I didn't order this."

"I did," a woman utters saucily from my left.

Twisting around, I find there's a cute brunette standing next to me.

The waitress, leaving the beer on the table, rolls her eyes and walks away.

Noticing the seat on my left is open, the girl nods to it and asks, "Mind if I sit down?"

Eh, what's the harm?

It's not like I'm going to go home with her.

"Go for it," I say, shrugging.

Plopping down, she adjusts her short, tight black skirt in a way that makes it ride up higher. I think that's done purposefully. Her top is black as well, like a leotard. And she tugs at the low neckline, smiling at me.

I look away, but when she flips her chestnut brown hair, practically hitting me with her long locks, my attention returns to her.

"I'm Mandy," she says.

"Hey, Mandy." I tip my bottle her way. "Thanks for the beer." I take a long pull, and once I set the bottle back down on the table, I tell her, "I'm Lars."

"I know," she replies, snickering.

Huh, she has really pretty green eyes.

Not like Becca's beautiful aqua-shaded ones, but still, they're nice.

But wait, she knows my name?

Huh?

Clearing my throat, I ask, "How do you know my name? Did you overhear us talking?"

"No." Mandy shakes her head, wavy hair bouncing. "I just happen to know you play for the Comets. Thus, I know who you are."

Wow, I can't believe she knows this.

It's not like our league is the NFL. Usually only our fans in our own cities know who we are.

Still feeling surprised, and also a little more than buzzed, I reply, "I do indeed play for the Comets. But how does a girl from Dover know that?"

Smiling smugly, she explains, "I'm not from Delaware. I'm actually from Columbus."

Ahh, now it all makes sense.

I nod. "Got it. But wait… You're saying you wouldn't have recognized me if you weren't from Ohio?" I pretend to be aghast. "You mean I'm not nationally known yet?"

I'm totally kidding, and she knows it.

Feigning a sad look, she replies, "Not yet, I'm afraid. But I bet someday you will be. The league you're in is growing. *And* you're really good."

"Wow, thanks."

Dropping her voice to a whisper, she says, "Can I tell you a secret?"

"Sure."

Mandy leans in a little closer, so close that I can smell her floral perfume. It's not entirely unpalatable.

Softly, she says, "You're hot enough that even if I hadn't recognized you, I still would've come over *and* bought you a beer."

Whoa.

Recognizing the need to tread carefully—*hey, I'm not too drunk to see that*—I brush her comment off by changing the subject.

"So, uh, what brings you to Delaware?"

My tactic works.

Moving away to a more respectable distance—*phew!*—Mandy says, "I'm visiting my aunt."

"That sounds nice."

Raising a brow, she asks, "Why are you in Dover?" She nods to the two guys still at the table, talking amongst themselves. "Is this like a football player gathering or something?"

I'm sure as hell not about to tell her I may end up here.

Nothing is a done deal yet.

And who knows who she could talk to.

So I just mutter, "It's something like that."

That seems to appease her.

Nodding, Mandy says, "You guys seem like you're having a lot of fun."

I shrug. "It's been okay."

Raising a brow, she asks, "Is it better now that I'm here?"

When I hold her gaze, she flutters her long lashes at me. Though she's trying to pretend she's kidding around, I sense Mandy is quite serious.

To be honest, it *is* better now that she's at the table. It was kind of getting boring with Mike talking to the safety and the other guys leaving to go to the bar to hit on women.

So yeah, this is better.

I answer honestly, "Yes. I'm having a better time now that you're here."

"Why, thank you," she says, looking pleased.

We talk for a little while longer, until I realize I have to pee like a racehorse.

"I think all the beer has caught up to me," I explain, standing. "Can you excuse me for a minute? I'm going to run to the men's room."

"Okay." Mandy points to my empty bottle. "Would you like for me to order you another beer?"

"Nah." I shake my head. "Just a glass of water would be fine." I point to her beer. "I still owe you a drink, though, so pick out whatever you want and have the waitress put it on my tab."

She lifts her bottle and takes a sip.

"Thanks," she says, setting her beer back down on the table. "But I think this will be my last one too. I'll just ask the waitress to bring us both water."

"Great," I say.

I head to the men's room, making my way through the thinning crowd.

Yeah, what the hell time is it, anyway?

It seems like I've been here forever.

I check my pocket for my phone, but realize I left it back on the table.

Eh, it can wait.

On my way into the men's room, I run into Mike.

"Hey," he says, propping open the door. "I noticed you met a new friend."

He chuckles knowingly, but he's dead wrong.

Waving my hand, I say, "It's not what you think. She's just someone to talk to and pass the time with. I mean, she seems nice. Cute too. But I have a serious girlfriend back home."

Mike appears unconvinced. "You might want to tell her that. I think she's really into you, dude." With a sly smile, he adds, "Are you sure you don't want *her* to drive you home?"

Is he crazy?

"Fuck, man, no way."

"Okay, just checking." He sighs. "In any case, I'm leaving soon."

"Hey, that's fine with me. I'll be ready to go once I get back to the table."

"Sounds good," he says, letting me grab hold of the door.

I head into the restroom, and he leaves.

Once I'm taking a leak, I think about what Mike said about Mandy being into me.

Fuck, I don't want to lead her on.

It is definitely time to go.

When I return to the table, Mandy shoots me a sour look.

"What's up?" I ask.

Huffing, she says, "It would've been nice if you'd told me you have a girlfriend."

I scowl over at Mike, and he shrugs. "Sorry, man, but she asked me point-blank. What was I supposed to say?"

He's right.

I'm not even really mad at him.

I just don't want to end this night on a bad note.

But it appears that it will end exactly like that.

Mandy, with a weird smirk I can't discern the meaning of, pushes her chair back roughly and stands.

"I'm out of here," she says. "And for the record, I hope you get hurt out on the field."

Jesus, that's harsh!

And I thought she was nice?

Clearly the beer and shots have messed with my judgment big-time.

At least I came out unscathed.

I pick up my phone and check for a text from Becca.

That's when I discover there are actually several from her.

But the one that stands out the most is the one she sent less than five minutes ago.

The one that says: **Go fuck yourself, Lars! WE'RE DONE!**

Chapter
THIRTY-THREE

Go Fuck Yourself, Lars!
Becca

Okay, obviously I can't sleep. I am far too worried about Lars.

As I toss and turn, I think about calling the hotel where he's staying and have them do a welfare check.

Is that too much?

I don't want to be one of those nutty, fly-off-the-handle-drama-type girlfriends.

But at two minutes to midnight, that's exactly what I'm about to become.

Then my phone dings.

It has to be Lars.

Finally!

Relief floods over me as I reach for the cell on my bedside table, muttering a grumpy, "It's about damn time."

I check the screen, and all my relief turns to instant fury.

Sitting up ramrod straight, I cry out, "What the hell? This can't be right."

But it is.

There are several texts from Lars's number.

But they're not any kind of sweet messages or even updates. They are freaking selfies of some bitch I've never seen before in my entire life.

She has long dark brown hair and big green eyes.

And she's smiling like she just got one over on someone—me.

Shaking, I unlock the phone so I can more thoroughly examine the pics from this unknown twit.

Let's see…

Here's a close-up of her with her full red lips puckered.

And one of her slinging back her hair, nose in the air like the bitch she so clearly is.

"Why in God's name would Lars send me photos of some duckface bimbo?"

I then scroll to the worst one, where this demon from hell—er, I mean chick—has her red lips wrapped around the neck of a beer bottle.

Great, this one has an accompanying text.

So much fun when the guy you plan to blow like this tonight— namely your boyfriend, you dumb bitch—lets you borrow his phone.

"*What?*" I roar, seeing red.

Lars is supposed to be out with the guys, not picking up a random woman and letting her text me this disgusting crap.

I look over the photos more closely.

It's clear they were taken at a bar.

So Lars is doing more than hanging out with the guys.

And to think I gave him my blessing!

A million thoughts run through my head.

Or at least it feels that way.

Maybe it's all a big misunderstanding?

Or maybe Lars really is out cheating?

Is murder legal?

Wait.

No, no it's not.

And that's not me, anyway.

Lars obviously just doesn't care.

He's not worth it.

Maybe he never did give a shit?

Why else would he let this bitch have access to his phone?

It would seem I was right all along in believing that it was all too good to be true. I mean, haven't I thought for a long time now that real love just isn't in the cards for me?

This proves it.

I've been had.

Choking up, I take a last look at the worst of the selfies, the one with the bottle.

Blowing out a disgusted breath, I think about calling Lars's stupid phone.

Maybe I can FaceTime him and catch him in the act.

But do I really want that?

No.

It's not worth it.

He's not worth it.

Instead of calling, I send one simple text that encapsulates exactly how I feel: **Go fuck yourself, Lars! WE'RE DONE!**

I turn off my phone.

And then I start to cry.

Chapter THIRTY-FOUR

Damage Control

Lars

I pick up my phone and stare at the cryptic text from Becca.

Go fuck yourself, Lars! WE'RE DONE!

Okay, I guess the message is not so cryptic.

Becca's words are pretty clear.

But why would she say that?

Mike asks me what's wrong.

He's standing next to where I'm seated, ready to go.

"I've been trying to get your attention," he says. "But you just keep staring at that thing like it's mesmerizing. Did you get some sort of bad news?"

Shaking my head, disgusted, I reply, "Yeah, you could say that."

He sits back down. "Hey, tell me what's up."

I run my hand down my face. "Remember that girlfriend I told you about?"

"Yeah."

"She just sent me this."

I hold up the phone so he can see Becca's text.

"Dude," he mutters. "Fuck, that's rough."

"Right?" I lower the phone.

"Jesus, what happened?"

I tell him, "I have no idea."

Tilting his head, he asks, "Did that message from your girl just come through?"

"Yeah," I confirm, double-checking the time. "Why?"

"Well, I hate to be the bearer of bad news, but I saw that chick you were talking to messing with a phone when you were in the men's room. I assumed it was hers, but maybe not."

"Whoa, what?"

Shit, now that I think about it, I did forget to lock my phone.

And now it's clear why Mandy was smirking at me when I returned from the bathroom.

I begin going through the full message thread from Becca.

Two seconds in, I'm exclaiming, "What the fuck?"

"What happened?" Mike asks.

"Dude…" I shake my head in disbelief. "You have got to see this shit."

Turning the phone to him, I show him how Mandy clearly hijacked my phone and texted a bunch of selfies to Becca. One particularly provocative pic includes a message on how Mandy plans to do to me what she's doing to the bottle.

When Mike sees that one, he says, "Holy hell, man. She actually sent that to your girlfriend?"

Feeling sick, I reply, "It would seem so."

"Fuck." He scoffs. "You are gonna have some major explaining to do."

"You got that right."

As I pocket my phone, he asks, "You ready to go?"

"Yeah, let's get out of here."

Man, I wish I'd never gone out in the first place. The sooner I get back to the hotel, the faster I can fix this.

In fact, I better start now.

Once I'm in the passenger seat of Mike's car, I call Becca.

But I'm sent straight to voice mail.

"Shit," I mutter.

Mike looks over at me. "She's not answering?"

"No. Her phone's turned off."

"That sucks."

"It sure does," I murmur quietly.

I'm hoping Becca is just making a statement and that she'll turn her phone back on soon. But even after Mike drops me off at the hotel and I'm back up in my room and in bed, every single attempt to reach her, I am sent straight to voice mail.

It's not what I want, but I finally do just leave a message.

"Hey, it's me. I saw what happened with my phone. Those selfies and that message, you know? Shit, of course you know. Anyway, it sounds lame, but the girl who sent that crap to you hijacked my phone while I was in the bathroom. Nothing happened, Becca, I swear. I just went out with the guys like I told you I was planning to do. She's just some girl that sat down at our table. I talked to her briefly, and that was it. Please call me back. We need to talk. I love—"

Beeeeep.

I'm cut off, having reached the maximum length for my message.

This fucking sucks.

I hate that I'm in Delaware.

I can't just drive over to Becca's house and fix this shit.

My phone is about to die, so I plug it into the charger.

I keep it by the bed, just in case Becca calls me back.

I guess I should try to get some sleep.

I still have practice tomorrow.

At least I'm not drunk anymore.

This sure has sobered me up. It's also made me reach a decision—I'm not going out with these guys for the rest of my stay.

It's going to be all work for me.

There's also going to be a lot of praying that my relationship can be saved.

Chapter
THIRTY-FIVE

A Tough but Necessary Decision
Becca

When I said I was done, I wasn't kidding.

I am finished with Lars.

One thing I learned while growing up with a bunch of brothers is how to take care of myself when it comes to men.

They would say things like "Don't give it up too fast, Becca" and "Make a man work for it."

They didn't mean just sex.

They wanted me to be careful with my heart.

Guess that's why I'm so cautious, though I sure slipped up with Lars.

I should've never put so much trust in him.

Another sage piece of advice passed down was to not allow myself to be walked all over.

It feels like Lars just did that.

Even if he didn't cheat—and really, how can I ever know for sure?—he let that nasty bimbo use his phone.

Okay, maybe he didn't actually give her consent. I realize that. But the fact she was able to access his cell long enough to take selfies *and* to send a rude message to me speaks volumes. I've told him a hundred times he should enable auto-lock on his phone.

In any case, Lars had to have been hanging with the girl.

I sigh as I roll to my side.

Yeah, I'm still in bed.

I don't need to be at work till noon since I stayed late yesterday with Skye.

I stare over at my phone on the bedside table, pondering what to do.

What should be my next move?

I don't know if I ever want to turn the phone back on.

I'd like to at least keep it turned off for a few days.

But that's not possible.

I need it for business.

"Crap." I sit up, bunching the covers around me as I reach over and grab the phone from the nightstand.

I power it on, rolling my eyes as soon as it springs to life.

Just as I suspected, there are numerous missed calls from Lars.

He even left a voice mail.

"Oh, lucky me," I grumble sarcastically.

I decide to listen to what he has to say, so I place the phone on speaker.

"Hey, it's me. I saw what happened with my phone. Those selfies and that message, you know? Shit, of course you know. Anyway, it sounds lame, but the girl who sent that crap hijacked my phone while I was in the bathroom. Nothing happened, Becca, I swear. I just went out with the guys like I told you I was planning to do. She was just some girl that sat down at our table. I talked to her briefly, and that was it. Please call me back. We need to talk. I love—"

He's cut off, having run out of time.

I blow out a breath as I tap the phone to my chin, thinking.

So the girl did take his phone.

But he somehow made that possible. He must've been talking with the girl if she was at their table.

How'd she know I was his girlfriend?

He either told her, or she had time to check out his texts.

It wouldn't have been hard to figure it out.

If Lars left his phone on the table when he went to the bathroom, that bimbo must have been sitting right next to him.

He did say he talked to her.

About what?

And what were they doing?

Flirting?

Thinking about hooking up?

I recall how Lars was no angel when I made a move on him at the theatre. He was more than ready to roll.

We haven't discussed specifics of his past all that much, but I know he's had some wild times.

Placing the phone back on the bedside table, I decide not to call him back.

Nor will I send him a text.

There's no point.

My mind is made up.

He's not getting away with making me look like a fool, damn it!

I tell myself Lars is probably going to leave town soon anyway.

Why drag it out?

But then a sob escapes me. "I just don't know what to do."

I'm torn.

Despite my better judgment, I listen to the message from him once more. Really it's just to hear his voice, and to drive the knife through my heart a little further.

I don't doubt that he loves me, but I can't live like this.

It's clear that if Lars is traded, our relationship will never work.

I'd always be questioning what he's up to.

So yeah, no, my text to him last night stands.

We are over.

Chapter THIRTY-SIX

Backing Off

Lars

I'm up half the night, waiting to hear from Becca.

We have to straighten this out.

Finally, when my phone remains silent, I fall asleep.

Morning comes, and the first thing I do is check it again.

"Fuck."

There's still no word from her.

Tired as hell, I somehow make it to practice on time.

I check my phone constantly as I suit up.

Still nothing.

I really think Becca might be done with me.

Tossing my phone into my temporary locker, I focus on football, going through the motions, running my routes, trying to shine for the Sharks.

But my heart isn't in it.

It hurts too much.

After practice, I leave Becca a few more voice mails, some texts too.

She ignores them all.

I almost call my agent to tell him I want to go home to Columbus. That way I can fix this horrible misunderstanding.

But I decide not to do that.

I'll leave Becca alone and give her time to cool down.

The next several days progress with me feeling like I'm in a daze.

My heart aches all the time.

Still, I continue to perform to the best of my abilities at each and every practice.

I'm a professional, and as they say, the show must go on.

I also hold out hope that I'll hear from Becca.

But every day my optimism is crushed.

Nonetheless, by the last day of practice, I'm back to believing I can save us.

I fly back to Columbus tomorrow. I'll formulate my next move with Becca then.

That's right, I'm not giving up.

She's had almost two weeks to cool down.

For the moment, though, I have one final practice to get through.

I put my thoughts aside and refocus on football.

With my new attitude and a light at the end of the tunnel, I perform spectacularly. I have three amazing receptions, one of which I run in for a touchdown.

On the sideline, Mike says, "You looked really good out there. I think you have a real chance with the Sharks."

I laugh. "Yeah, I guess I do."

For a moment, it dawns on me that I could come here unattached. Sure, I'd need to sell my house back in Columbus. But if things don't work out with Becca, meaning I can't win her back, I have to ask myself what's really keeping me in Columbus?

Wait, I don't want that.

I want Becca.

Mike asks, "Do you want to play here? Are you hoping the trade goes through?"

Shit, I have no clue.

Shrugging, I try to blow it off.

But he looks at me pointedly.

I ignore that too.

Once we're in the locker room, taking off our equipment, the subject of Becca is brought up again.

Mike, seated next to me, yanks his pads over his head. Running his hand through his sweaty dark hair, he says, "I'm guessing you still haven't heard from your girl?"

I shake my head. "No, not a thing."

Looking thoughtful, he says, "You know, sometimes women need to work these things out on their own schedule. Unfortunately, it doesn't always match up with ours."

I snort, "That's for sure. And trust me, I've been telling myself that same thing ever since this happened."

"You giving her time still?"

"I am."

Mike finishes undressing and wraps a towel around his waist.

Standing, he pats my shoulder. "Hey, don't give her too much time, though. It could go the other way. She could reach a point where she thinks you don't care. It's a difficult balance, my friend."

"Jeez, you're just full of sunny optimism," I quip sarcastically.

He shrugs. "I just try to see it from all sides."

"I know." I sigh. "I've been thinking the same thing."

"Don't think too long, though," he warns. "I think I'd get on it as soon as you get back."

He is so right.

But I don't have time to tell Mike I already made that decision.

As he heads off to the showers, I remain seated on the locker room bench.

Yeah, no way am I giving up on Becca.

I caught her once.

I can catch her again.

I think about how my girl is a runner.

I know that.

She ran from me at the theatre.

And she ran from "us" in the beginning.

She's just running from me again now.

Good thing making great catches is what I do.

And no doubt about it, winning Becca back would be my greatest reception of all time.

Chapter THIRTY-SEVEN

What a Jerk!

Becca

Over the next couple of weeks, I keep my butt busy with work. Lars is far from my mind.

Ha!

Who am I kidding?

The stupid ass is all I think about.

And let me assure you, he is an ass.

So much for making all my dreams come true.

Liar!

Apart from a flurry of voice mails and texts the day after the incident, I don't hear another word from him.

"What a jerk!" I look over at Jodi, poised for her reaction.

I've just shared with her all the anger and fury I've been feeling.

But she's just sitting there, not saying a thing.

Huh?

When she continues to not respond, I prompt, "Am I right?"

She shrugs. "Yeah, Becca, I guess you are."

Balling up a piece of paper and lobbing it over at her, I snap, "What do you mean 'you guess'? Whose side are you on, anyway? We should be bashing Lars together."

Intercepting the paper ball easily, she replies, "I don't know about that. I'm on your side, of course. But let's review."

"Okay."

"Didn't you tell Lars you're done with him?"

"Um, yeah."

"Yet he still left messages, right?"

"Only for a day," I snap, trying to generate some outrage.

"Did you respond to any of those messages?"

"Er, uh, no."

Jodi throws up her hands. "Then what is the guy supposed to think, Becca?"

Looking down at my desk, I mutter, "I don't know."

"You told him to leave you alone. But he still tried. I think when you didn't respond, he decided to respect your wishes."

Damn it, she has a point.

"I hate when you're right." Still feeling defiant, I add, "But the jerk shouldn't have given up so easily. I don't want him to respect my wishes, damn it!"

Jodi snorts. "What kind of modern-woman approach is that?"

"Okay, okay, I don't know." I let out a long sigh. "I guess a part of me just really *wants* to hear from him."

In a soft, understanding tone, she says, "That part would be your heart."

I place my head in my hands. "Ugh, you're right again. I hate this so much."

Wheeling her chair over, Jodi wraps a comforting arm around my shoulders. "I know, sweetie." She leans the side of her head against mine. "This is a tough situation, no doubt. Your heart is warring with your head."

"That's for sure."

The tears begin to fall.

I let it all out—my grief, my pain.

And then I straighten in my chair.

Moving her arm from around my shoulders, Jodi reaches for the box of tissues I keep on my desk.

Grabbing a bunch, she hands them to me. "Here," she says. "You look like you can use a few."

"Thanks." I sniffle into one tissue while wiping my cheeks with another.

Patting my arm, Jodi says, "I really hate seeing you hurting like this."

"Trust me—" I blow my nose. "—I hate *feeling* like this. No man has ever had me this messed up."

With sadness in her pretty whiskey-brown eyes, she says softly, "That's because you've never been in love like this before."

"Actually, I've never been in love like this or in any way. I thought maybe I was in the past, but I know now it was something else, like infatuation… or lust. Lars has shown me what real love is."

That brings on a fresh round of tears.

Once I pull myself together, Jodi quietly suggests, "Maybe you two should get together and talk once he's back in town. He comes home tomorrow, right?"

"Yes. His two weeks in Dover are done."

She nudges me. "Then get in touch with him. Make a move. I think you made your point of how angry you were with how long you've ignored him."

I'm hesitant, though.

"I just don't know," I hedge. "What if he does get traded?"

Sternly, Jodi says, "Stop. I'm tired of hearing about that. If he does, he does. You two will work it out. Be an adult, Becca."

"Yeesh." I blink over at her. "You're tough."

"I think you need a little tough love right about now."

I murmur, "Maybe I do."

"So when are you going to call Lars?"

"I don't know. Not yet."

Jodi's not giving up.

Nor do I expect her to.

She knows what's best for me.

"Don't be so stubborn," she says.

"I'm trying not to be," I whine. "I just can't make a decision right this instant."

Jodi sighs. "Look. Why don't you take tomorrow off? That'll give you time to think with a clear head."

I nod. "Okay."

She has a point.

Why argue?

Jodi also has a warning. "Becca, seriously, make a decision. Don't wait too long. You don't want to throw away the best thing to ever come along in your life. Lars is everything you've ever wanted in a man. How many times have you told me that? Not to mention, he really does love you."

Crap, every fiber in my being knows she's right.

But all I can do is just sit here and nod.

Hey, at least I'm not running.

Yet.

Chapter
THIRTY-EIGHT

Next Moves
Lars

I fly back to Columbus, ready and pumped to win Becca back.

Yeah, I got this.

Only problem is every time I call her, I'm sent to voice mail, just like before when I was in Dover.

Fuck!

I don't bother with texts.

We need to resolve this with spoken words, not typed statements.

So the first day and night that I'm home, I leave many messages for Becca, begging for her to call me back.

I hear nothing in return.

But I'm not deterred.

In fact, I start leaving voice mails again on day number two early in the morning, as soon as I wake up.

I continue into the afternoon.

In the middle of one particularly long apology, my agent beeps through.

Switching over, I take his call.

"Hey, what's up?"

"Actually, not much," he replies.

"What's that supposed to mean? Why are you calling me if you have no news?"

"I didn't say I don't have any news, Lars. It's just not groundbreaking."

What a tool.

"Would you just get to the point?" I grind out.

He finally does.

"The deal is dead, my man."

"How do you mean?"

"The Sharks aren't making any moves after all. Management mentioned something about budgetary constraints that hadn't been taken into account."

I muse, "I thought their offer was a bit generous."

"You don't sound upset," my agent notes.

"Fuck, I'm not. This is great news."

He just chuckles.

A sense of relief washes over me, and the first person, the only person, I want to talk to and share this fabulous news with is Becca.

First, though, I need a little more info. I have to know if the Comets are done with trying to trade me.

"So what happens now?" I ask. "You talked to the Sharks, but have you spoken with the Comets?"

"Yes, Lars, I have."

"And?"

"They want to keep you."

I release a breath I didn't realize I was holding. "They do? Are you sure? The Comets will keep me even with my high salary?"

"Yes, yes, and yes." My agent laughs. "The answer to all those questions is a resounding yes."

"You're absolutely sure about this?"

"I am."

"Shit, okay. Let's discuss all the details later. There's someone I need to call."

My agent lets me go, and I start to call Becca.

But my finger just kind of hovers over the screen.

What if she's still not answering?

Is she even checking her messages?

"Maybe not," I murmur.

I have a better idea.

Yeah, this is good.

With a renewed sense of urgency, and feeling fucking awesome, I pocket my phone and grab my car keys.

Avoiding me by phone is too easy for Becca.

She can hide.

But she can't run from me in person.

Even if she does, I'm faster.

Chapter
THIRTY-NINE

Holding Out
Becca

*L*ars is back in town, and he's calling me like crazy.

I don't answer, but that doesn't stop him from leaving multiple voice mails.

I don't listen to any of them.

I'm still thinking and trying to decide what I want to do.

I will make a decision, just like I told Jodi I would, but I'm not sure when.

I'm holding out, and I really don't know why.

I love Lars.

Maybe I'm just trying to punish him?

By the time Friday rolls around, his attempts to get ahold of me ramp up.

I'm caving.

Still, I'm not quite there yet.

I'm not ready to talk to him.

But when I come upon a sports update on my phone, everything changes.

It reads: **Comets Will Be Keeping Wide Receiver Lars Samuels, Putting Trade Rumors to Rest.**

Holy crap!

Lars is staying with the team.

He's *not* leaving.

My heart soars.

Wait, why is my heart soaring?

I haven't decided what I want to do, right?

Or maybe I have.

"Damn it!"

Jumping up, I realize I need to get out of the house.

I'm going crazy with my own back-and-forth.

I have to go somewhere, anywhere, just not here.

Slipping my phone into the back pocket of my skinny jeans, I smooth down the soft pink cashmere sweater I have on and head out.

Once in my car, I feel the urge to run.

But I hold off.

You are bigger than this, Becca.

To tamp down my escape instinct, I aimlessly drive around for a while.

It's soothing.

The hum of the car and the radio playing lightly in the background are relaxing to me.

I even start thinking more clearly.

I consider driving over to Lars's house, but the turns I make don't lead me there.

Instead, I find myself at the old quaint theatre where he and I first met.

I drive by the front slowly.

The marquee indicates there's an old eighties John Cusack movie playing, *Say Anything.*

"I love that movie," I say out loud.

It starts at seven.

On the dash, I check the time.

It's six thirty.

I can do this.

I have time.

I can see the movie and then head over to Lars's place.

Am I just stalling?

Maybe.

But I need a time-out.

All the parking spaces in front of the theatre are taken, so I drive around to an alley in the back and park there.

After an adjustment of my long ponytail, I hop out of the car.

I'm sure the movie will make me cry, especially the scene where Lloyd Dobler holds up that boom box outside Diane Court's bedroom window, blasting Peter Gabriel's "In Your Eyes."

Damn it, I *need* to see that.

I need to see that true love does exist.

And that things can work out, even in the face of adversity.

Desperately Seeking Becca
Lars

I'm assuming Becca is working today, so I drive over to the bridal shop.

Unfortunately, I find the door locked and the sign turned to Closed.

It's not that late, is it?

I check my phone.

Damn, it's after five.

It makes sense that the shop would be closed by now, especially on a Friday.

After hopping back into the Nav, I drive out to Becca's house.

It's such a beautiful day. The skies are blue and the birds are chirping. It gives me hope that I can save my relationship.

But my hope is allayed when I pull up her long gravel driveway only to find she's not home.

"Fuck," I bite out. "This is so frustrating."

Becca doesn't have a garage, and her car's not here, so it's pretty obvious she's out.

Just to be sure, I hop out of my car and walk up to her door.

After knocking and receiving no response, I head around to the back to see if maybe she's out on the porch, a place that means a lot to us.

I'm leaving no stone unturned.

What if Becca had car trouble and Jodi dropped her off?

I'm considering everything here.

But she's not on the back porch.

Our chairs, nudged close together like they haven't been moved since the last time we were out here, just about knocks me on my ass. A barrage of memories of us sitting in these very same spots, sipping iced tea and talking late into the night, overwhelms me.

I need a minute.

"Damn."

Collapsing down to one of the chairs, I place my head in my hands.

I didn't truly realize just how much I miss Becca.

This is bad.

This is ripping-your-heart-out level stuff.

I sit for a while, just pulling my shit together.

I consider staying until she returns, but I don't want to freak her out.

Last thing I need is for her to think I've turned into a damn stalker.

But maybe that ship has sailed.

Because here I am, hanging out on her back porch while she's not home.

Standing, I prepare to leave.

I'll just come back.

I look around and sigh.

We have got to make this work.

I have to get her back.

Once I return to my vehicle, I head back up the long driveway.

What should I do now?

Where should I go?

I need to waste time before returning.

And you bet your ass I'll be back.

Nothing can change my mind now.

For old time's sake, I decide to drive over to the old theatre where Becca and I first met. The little town where it's located isn't far.

That means I reach my destination quickly.

"Hey, *Say Anything* is playing," I murmur to myself when I see the marquee.

Someone is pulling out of a spot right out in front, so I wait and pull in once they're gone.

Yep, I'm going in.

I need to waste a little time to allow Becca a chance to return home anyway, right?

The movie will be a good distraction.

I'll swing by her place afterward.

I check the clock on the dash and find it's five to seven.

"Shit, the movie starts in five minutes. I better get my ass in there."

I head inside and buy a ticket in the lobby.

Just for the hell of it—and mostly to remind me of Becca—I purchase a big tub of buttered popcorn from the concession stand.

Once I'm inside the theatre itself, it takes me a few seconds for my eyes to adjust to the darkness.

The previews are playing, providing the only real illumination.

I forgot how dark this place is.

As I start down the aisle, I think about where I should sit. It's not like the place is super crowded or anything, but there are more people in attendance than there were last time I was here.

I walk a few rows down, and then stop.

That's when I hear a gasp from the back of the theatre, an all too familiar gasp.

Joy fills my heart as I spin around.

I see her, even in the darkness.

I'd know her anywhere.

Yes, there she is in the back row, right where we sat on Valentine's Day.

Softly, I murmur, "Becca?"

I take one step in her direction, praying she doesn't get up and run.

Chapter FORTY-ONE

History Rewritten
Becca

*H*oly crap!

Lars just walked into the theatre.

What's the chance?

I let out a gasp of surprise.

I think he hears me.

Why else is he turning around?

Even from a few rows away, that electricity that always runs between us sparks to life.

It's only been a little over two weeks since I last saw him, but it feels like forever.

I thought I was doing sort of okay without him.

Ha!

How could I have been so blind?

I was sadly mistaken.

This man gives me life.

I feel more alive now, my senses more acute, especially when it comes to him.

I guess that's why I can hear him when he says, "Becca?"

I swear I even smell the popcorn he's holding.

I smile at him, and he smiles back.

Damn, Lars is more gorgeous than ever.

I forgot how he takes my breath away.

I love every part about him, from his messy chestnut-brown hair, his deep-set dark eyes, his strong jaw, his aquiline nose, all the way down to his good heart.

I glance down, appreciating how his dark blue jeans hug his strong quads, and how the forest green pullover he has on is snug enough to beautifully show off his wide shoulders and bulging biceps.

I need him near me now!

I start to beckon him over to join me in the last row, but he's already on his way.

Guess he feels the same way I do.

On the big screen, the previews are wrapping up.

Who cares?

My focus is solely on Lars.

When he reaches me, despite the fact that he stops a few seats away, my body starts buzzing.

I'm shaking, just like Lloyd Dobler in the back seat of the car with Diane.

How ironic is it that this is the movie we've both come to see?

What brought him here?

He couldn't have seen my car since I parked in the back.

And why would Lars be on this side of town anyway?

Is this just meant to be?

Did fate lead him here?

Did it lead me?

I ask myself if there are ever really any accidents.

I don't think so.

He clears his throat, and I look up at him.

We have so much to say.

But now is not the time.

We just need to live in this moment.

We need to go with the flow.

We need to get back to us.

He knows it.

I know it.

Raising a brow, Lars utters the words I said to him the night we met. "You don't mind if I sit here in this last row with you, do you?"

I nod.

He smirks and adds, "I don't mean *with you,* with you, of course. It's just that I get vertigo if I sit too close to the screen."

Snickering, I reply, "Well, this is definitely not close."

"No." He smiles. "It's not."

I can't believe he remembers our conversation so well, almost word by word.

I can't believe I remember it too.

I do, though, so I say, "I don't mind the company."

His eyes tell me he knows what we're doing—we're rewriting our past.

Maybe in doing so, we can recoup what we lost?

"Cool. Thanks," he says.

Lars sits a couple of seats away, just like I did that fateful night.

Extending the cardboard tub of popcorn he's holding, he gives it a little shake.

Trying not to laugh, he says, "I'm open to sharing."

I raise a hand, holding in my own great big grin. "No thanks, I'm good."

"Whatever." Pretending to be offended, he pulls away the popcorn and snaps, "Suit yourself."

Ooh, he's good at this game.

But I am too.

"It's just that I don't like it."

"Like what?" Lars says, following the script that was written so long ago, acting as if he has no clue.

"Popcorn." I motion to the bucket in his lap. "I'm not a fan."

"Oh."

He smiles over at me.

The theatre dims even more, almost to full darkness, as the movie begins. Lars and I look at the screen, and it's like we know we won't reenact the parts of our conversation that were about the movie playing Valentine's night, as this one is different. Nor do we mention anything about snow, seeing as it's May.

He does lean toward me, though.

So I pick up our trip to the past there.

Patting the seat next to me, I say, "You should move over here."

He shrugs. "Okay."

"Cool."

Once Lars is seated next to me, he sets the popcorn tub on the floor.

Oooh, I know what comes next.

Trying to appear nonchalant, I drape an arm around the back of his seat.

He moves closer, his knee touching mine.

The electricity reaches insane heights, just like it did that night, and I murmur, "Beautiful."

Out of the blue—totally deviating from the script, though in the best possible way—Lars snatches me up in his strong, capable arms so quickly that I barely know what's happening.

He then starts kissing me furiously.

Finally!

Chapter
FORTY-TWO

A Sexy Detour

Lars

*B*ecca and I have been playing a game, one we obviously both like. We are echoing the lines we uttered to each other the night we first met.

But I'm in her role.

And she's in mine.

Our reenactment reaches a point where it must become a different story, though—a better one, one with a new outcome.

That's why I don't just tentatively press my lips to hers, like she did to me that first night. No, I fucking take charge, snatching Becca up in my arms like she's a rag doll and kissing her like my life depends on it.

It just may.

Perhaps it does for her too, as she lets out a gasp, pulling back to breathe me in.

But just as quickly, she's kissing me just as enthusiastically.

It's exhilarating.

My soul heals as I drink her in. Becca is honeysuckles and soft woman, like in the beginning.

No, wait, she's much more now.

She's the woman I love more than anything in the world.

How could I have ever entertained a life without her, even if it was only for a minute?

Becca and I have so much to discuss, but it can wait.

We need this reprieve.

This is how we'll rebuild.

Our rewrite continues, with me stopping long enough to ask, "Do you want to get out of here?"

This time, she doesn't run.

I welcome this deviation from source material, smiling at her like a mofo.

Snickering, she says, "Let's go to my house. It's closer."

Chuckling, I say, "I like the way you think."

This rewrite is on.

As we stand, we're met with a few disapproving stares from the folks who are close enough to have witnessed our steamy make-out session.

They'll live.

"Guess we're more interesting than the movie," Becca whispers to me.

"Guess so," I reply a little louder than necessary.

One woman scoffs, and then we get the hell out of there.

Once we're out on the sidewalk, I nod to my SUV. "I can drive. You can just leave your car." I glance around. "Where is it, anyway?"

"It's in the back alley," Becca says.

"Ah, okay. We'll pick it up in the morning. Is that okay with you?"

Stepping over to the passenger side of the Navigator, she says, "That's more than okay with me."

We don't want to separate, even if it is just to take our own vehicles to her house.

We're together now, and together we must stay.

There is still more healing to do, healing that starts inside the Nav.

I barely have the engine running before Becca is reaching over the console, running her hand up my jean-clad leg.

Closer, closer…

Chuckling, I warn, "You better stop what you're doing or we may not make it to your house."

She raises a brow. "Who says we have to, Lars?"

"Christ, you're killing me, woman."

"Just drive," Becca demands, moving her hand up until it's covering my cock.

That gets me rolling.

I've never been so glad this little town is so tiny. Nor have I ever been as happy that the route to Becca's house is desolate and tree-lined.

As we travel down a lonely country road, Becca rubs my dick through my jeans, making me longer and harder.

"We should stop somewhere," she breathes, as desperate for more contact as I am.

"Where do you suggest we go?" I ask.

Hey, I'm more than game to continue this somewhere more private.

I don't think we're going to make it to her house.

Pointing to a break in the trees up ahead, she says, "There's an old dirt road that leads down to a lake just up there a bit. It used to be a fishing spot, but no one ever goes there anymore. It's overgrown and the road is in disrepair. I think we can manage, though."

"Ah, no worries." Patting the dash, I say confidently, "We'll make it down that road in this."

"I think we will, Lars," she coos.

"And when we do…"

Leaning over to trail kisses down along my neck, she says, "I'm thinking the exact same thing."

Chapter
FORTY-THREE

There Is Nowhere Else I'd Rather Be

Becca

Lars turns onto the dirt road I direct him to as darkness descends.

The old country lane is bumpy and rutted, like I told him it would be, but his vehicle handles it adeptly, just as we knew it would.

"I told you the ole Nav would come through," he says, winking over at me.

God, he is beautiful.

And he doesn't even know it, not really.

As we travel down the gravelly lane at a snail's pace, thick weeds and greenery brush along the sides.

I barely notice, as I'm too anxious and excited. I guess that's why it feels like it's taking forever to reach the lake.

But then I see it, a silvery mirror against the nighttime sky.

I only take it in briefly, as I can't keep my hands—or lips—off Lars.

Not that he's stopping me.

Undoing his jeans, I slip my hand inside.

He hits the brakes and we come to a full stop. "Damn, woman."

I look up.

It's so pretty, the scene before us. The lake is like a picture, calm and still. There's a big full moon up in the dark sky, a sky blanketed in a million twinkling stars.

Leaning my head on Lars's shoulder, still stroking him, I whisper, "I love you."

"I love you too," he tells me, kissing the top of my head.

We have so much to talk about, but it can wait.

Expressing our love is all that matters right now.

He undoes his seat belt, and with my free hand, I rid myself of mine.

He then moves his seat back, and I crawl over the console to straddle him.

Placing my hands on either side of his face, I tell him, "I've missed you so much."

Wrapping his arms around me, he pulls me in as close as he can. "Not as much as I've missed you, Becca."

Beneath me, I feel how damn hard he is.

Pressing down onto him, eliciting a husky groan, I murmur, "I can tell."

Turning serious, Lars urges me back so he can see my face.

Peering into my eyes, he says quietly, "We have a lot to talk about. I know that. But the only thing that needs to be put out there right now is that I want you in my life. You can run to the ends of the Earth, sweetheart, but I think you know I will never quit chasing you." He tells me that he was looking for me, and how he stopped by my house. "I sat out back for a while, just thinking about us."

"I was going to try and find you tonight too," I whisper. "I was just building up the courage. That's why I stopped at the theatre, to strengthen my resolve. I was planning to drive straight over to your house directly after."

"Yeah?"

He doesn't look totally convinced, and I think I know what he needs to hear.

Softly, I say, "I'm sorry, Lars. I want you to know something—I'm done running. Unless, of course…" I brush back a swath of dark hair from his forehead. "It's with you."

"How do you mean, unless it's with me?"

Running my hand along his stubbled cheek, I explain, "I mean if you ever are traded to another team, I'll go with you. I will run *with* you, not away from you."

Raising a brow, he asks, "What about your business and your life here?"

"There is no life without you." I take a deep breath before exhaling slowly. And then I continue, "I'm sure Jodi and I would work something out. Maybe I'd just open another bridal consulting shop in a different city. It could be like a franchise, or an expansion."

"You wouldn't miss working directly with her? I mean, shit, you two are a team."

"Not as much as you and I are," I reply. "Jodi knows that too."

Shaking his head, Lars says, "You amaze me, woman. I love you so fucking much."

I press my forehead to his. "I love you too, you gorgeous man."

What started out as desperate now becomes tender and soft. Lars lifts my hand from his face and kisses my palm.

Raising the hem of my sweater, he tugs it up and over my head, interrupting our make-out session only for a beat.

His shirt is next.

And then my bra.

My skin next to his feels like heaven.

It's been far too long.

I kiss Lars with renewed enthusiasm.

And beneath my lips, I feel him smile.

But then he's back to moving his lips with mine.

We're synchronized in our movements, even as he helps me take off my jeans, my panties discarded along with them.

And then it's his turn.

I tug down his jeans and boxers with his help.

When his cock springs free, I'm on him. He works my clit until I'm so wet that he slips right in.

We gasp, our eyes meeting.

"Fuck, Becca."

"I know, right?"

He feels unbelievably amazing.

I hope I do for him too.

I think I may, based on how he's swallowing hard and closing his eyes.

"Is it okay to move?" I ask softly.

"Yeah…" He blows out a breath. "Just go slowly for a minute."

Lars is usually so controlled.

I kind of love that I can make him falter.

But his loss of control doesn't last for long.

Soon he's back to his usual self, lifting me and working me up and down his length with skill.

"Come for me, Becs," he urges.

I can't even speak as pleasure floods through me.

I expect Lars to follow in his release, but he holds off, working me up to another crashing crescendo.

My legs are shaking, my vision blurred as I collapse against his strong chest. "Let go," I whisper.

He does, and I feel him explode.

For a long time afterward, we just hold onto each other, listening to our mingled heartbeats and breaths.

A solace comes over me at that moment.

I'm no longer worried about anything.

I know that we are truly together, as one, stronger than ever.

What I told Lars is true—I will never run from him ever again.

He's finally caught me.

But there's nowhere else I'd rather be.

EPILOGUE

Forever Promises

Lars

*I*n the days ahead, so much happens.

First, Becca and I finally have that talk we put off.

So much is resolved. We work out *all* of our misunderstandings. I apologize to her for what Mandy did—absconding my phone and texting those stupid selfies and the rude text to her.

Becca, shaking her head, replies, "Lars, stop. I'm not even mad about that any longer."

We're hanging in our favorite spot, seated on the Adirondack chairs on her back porch, drinking iced tea on a beautiful June evening.

Crickets are chirping, and the sun has painted the sky in beautiful shades of red, orange, and purple.

"I know you're not," I say, sighing. "But I still feel bad about it."

Reaching over and taking my hand, Becca says, "Well, don't. I'm fine. It's all in the past, so let's leave it there."

I squeeze her hand. "Sounds good to me. And I couldn't agree more. In fact, I've been thinking about something."

"Ooh, do tell," she says, cocking her head as she peers over at me.

"I've been thinking about us," I state quietly. "And what lies ahead."

"Ahh, so we're moving from the past to the future now?"

"We are indeed. Isn't that what it's all about? Moving forward?"

"It is," Becca agrees, swinging our interlocked hands between us. Shooting me a sly smile, she adds, "Only thing is my definition of moving forward has changed significantly."

I think I know where this is going, but I still have to ask, "How do you mean?"

She stops swinging our hands but doesn't let go.

I like that.

It shows me that she's growing more comfortable in expressing her feelings.

Taking a deep breath, she explains, "I used to view 'moving forward' as running away. You know that."

"Do I ever."

"Lars!" Becca lets go of my hand so she can smack my forearm. "Be serious here."

"Okay, okay, I am. I'll be good."

Turning her chair to face me, she goes on, "I don't see it that way anymore. I told you the night we reunited that I'm never going to run from you, not ever again. And I won't."

I murmur softly, "I believe you."

She nods.

But now it's time for me to turn my chair to face her.

I have something important to ask Becca Nadeau.

"So about this new definition of moving forward…"

"Yes?" She raises a brow.

Sucking in a breath and releasing it quickly, I say in a rush of words, "I think we should get married."

Her beautiful aqua eyes widen. "What?"

I fumble in the pocket of the light jacket I have on for something I bought earlier today—a beautiful sparkling round diamond solitaire engagement ring.

I know this is Becca's dream ring, because I confirmed it with Jodi. I also found out Becca's ring size from her. Jodi was ecstatic, but I made her promise not to say a thing to Becca. Good thing she's really good at keeping a secret.

I can tell from Becca's expression when I pop open the little black velvet box that she never saw this one coming.

Dropping down to one knee, I ask, "Will you marry me, Becca?"

She swallows hard, and then the tears come.

I can tell they're happy ones.

"Yes," she murmurs. And then louder, she says, "Yes, yes, yes, Lars, I will marry you."

"Woohoo!" I cry out.

She falls into my arms, but I stop her for a sec. "Wait, we're forgetting something."

She pulls back. "What?"

Taking her left hand and slipping the ring onto her ring finger, I say, "This."

That makes Becca smile, and then she begins to laugh.

It's the most joyful sound.

I quietly share what's in my heart. "You just made me the happiest man on this planet."

"I hope I can always make you happy," she says. "Because you just did what you long ago promised—you've made all my dreams come true."

"I always will, my love," I promise. "Forever."

The End

Up next in the bestselling Men of Fall football romance series is Zane's story in *Down by Contact,* releasing June 2021.

And in the bestselling Boys of Winter hockey romance books, look for Landen's story, *Bet on Ice*, releasing January 2021.

About The Author

S.R. Grey is a USA Today Bestselling Author of the popular Boys of Winter hockey books and Men of Fall football novels. Both series can be read in any order or as standalones. Other New Adult and Romantic Suspense works of hers include the Judge Me Not books, the Promises series, the Inevitability duology, A Harbour Falls Mystery trilogy, and the Laid Bare series of novellas.

Ms. Grey resides in Pennsylvania. When not writing, she can be found reading, traveling, running, or cheering for her hometown sports teams, sometimes all at the same time.

Visit S.R. Grey's Author Website (if for nothing else, because it's pretty!):
srgrey.com

S.R. Grey on Facebook is a hoot:
www.facebook.com/SRGrey

S.R. Grey's FB Reading Group is even more fun:
www.facebook.com/groups/SRGreyHardAbsandHotBooks/

Sign-up to receive her exciting Author Newsletter (you know you want to):
mad.ly/signups/106801/join

Follow S.R. Grey on BookBub for selected Sales Updates:
www.bookbub.com/authors/s-r-grey

Follow S.R. Grey on Twitter for randomness:
twitter.com/AuthorSRGrey

Follow S.R. Grey on Instagram for the riveting pics (well, at least she thinks so):
www.instagram.com/authorsrgrey/

S.R. Grey Goodreads Author page:
www.goodreads.com/author/show/6433082.S_R_Grey

Wait!

It's not over yet.

Read the first chapter of **Forward Progress**, the first standalone novel in the bestselling *Men of Fall* series.

Chapter
ONE

Leaving Las Vegas
Graham

I hesitate, my pen hovering over the yellow sheet of legal paper on my desk as I contemplate what to write.

What am I doing?

I'm making a list of what I'd like to achieve throughout the second half of this year. But damn, it's no easy task.

I want to get this done, though. The rehab I went through a couple of years ago made me a big believer in things like setting goals and writing out lists.

My brain is usually racing when I write these kinds of things. I have so much to get down on paper that my pen moves too fast, leaving my sentences a jumbled blur of words I have to decipher later.

Today, however, I've got nothing.

Maybe because all my most recent goals have been achieved... and therefore checked off.

Like this one—I wanted to have my own gym business *and* make it a raging success.

Check, check.

Both of those objectives have been achieved.

And then there's my ongoing goal of always trying to give back and help others.

Check that off too.

I'm still an active sponsor for Narcotics Anonymous, even if it is only for one guy these days—Las Vegas Wolves hockey player Benjamin Perry.

Still counts, though, right?

Ah, but Perry hardly needs me anymore. He's doing really well on his own.

In the past, I always had my sister, Chloe, to worry about. She wasn't in NA or anything, but she had her share of troubles in the relationship department. Seemed I was always swooping in to rescue her.

But she met and married someone great—Dylan Culderway, another hockey player I'm friends with. Chloe now has a calm and happy life. She and Dylan even have a baby on the way.

Fuck, I can't wait to be an uncle.

I spend a few minutes wondering if their baby will have dark blonde hair and cerulean blue eyes like my sister and I do, or if she'll have brown eyes and dark hair like Dylan.

Oh hell, I'm just stalling.

"Get to work on that list, Graham," I mutter to myself to conjure up some motivation. "There has to be at least *one* important thing you have yet to achieve."

And there is.

But it's the one goal I've resisted writing down, on this or any prior lists.

Maybe because this goal is the most important of all and putting it down on paper gives it life. That means it's something I'll *have* to achieve.

No excuses.

"Just write it down, dumbass," I hiss. "Do it. It's the one thing you've wanted more than anything these past three years."

What is this big goal?

It's to play professional football again.

Shit, it's out there now.

I mean, I can't unthink it.

"But what if I *can't* play like I once did?" I whisper, like that would be the worst thing in the world.

Hell, it would.

Other thoughts race through my mind...

What if my once promising football career is really and truly over? What if I'm washed up?

Do you see now why I'm afraid to write down this goal?

"But you were good." I touch pen to paper, willing my hand to move. "No, you were fucking great, Graham Tettersaw."

It's true, I was. I had a completion percentage in the 65 percent range, and I passed for over 3000 yards every season I played.

I also averaged 30+ touchdowns a year, meaning I was rarely intercepted.

Not to mention, the fans fucking loved me.

I was a god, damn it!

But then I got hurt, and a god I was no more. I was just a man, a man with a blown knee and a crappy attitude. Hence the prescription drug addiction. I just didn't care.

The team I was playing for at the time—the Arizona Cardinals—cut my ass. Doctors, really good ones, told me I'd never play again.

Down in the dumps about, well, just about everything, I developed that nasty painkiller addiction.

That led me to NA.

It worked, and I got clean and sober.

I still am—painkiller-free for over three years now.

That's why I like to give back as a sponsor. It's the least I can do. I believe if I can overcome addiction, anyone can.

"So what would everyone you've helped want you to do now?" I ask myself out loud.

I know the answer. It's simple, really.

They'd want me to believe in myself as much as I believed in them.

That finally gets the pen moving and I write down the one goal that means the world to me—I want to play professional football again.

Shit, that feels good.

On a roll, I jot down another—I'd like to be picked up by a good team.

Problem with that is I'm thirty years old. I'll actually be thirty-one this September, which is only four months away.

There's not much call for a quarterback in his early thirties, especially if he's been out of the game for a few years.

But I have a few things going for me…

I've kept myself in great shape. And I just landed a slick new agent.

I made that move after I discovered the one I had the past few years wasn't even trying anymore.

This new one, Jock Sosarelli, is fantastic. He represents a ton of sports figures, including some of my hockey pals. Brent Oliver is one of his clients. He's the biggest star for the Las Vegas Wolves, so that's something right there.

Jock is good, really good.

A middle-aged former professional athlete, the guy knows sports. Jock used to play baseball, like a hundred years ago.

Okay, not that long ago, but I like to tell him that.

Good thing he takes it well.

Another reason why Jock is a good fit for me is because an injury ended his career too. He understands the perils I face. That's probably why he was quick to pick me up as a new client. I think he'd like to see me get the second chance he never did.

My cell phone rings, breaking me from my reverie. And wouldn't you know it, it's Jock. He wants to FaceTime, so this must be good news.

Leaning back in the chair in my office, I hold the phone up.

Jock's silver-streaked black hair and smiling mug fill the screen.

"Hey, what's up?" I say.

"A lot," he replies. "And you're going to love this news, Tettersaw."

"Hmm…" I'm curious, but first I feel compelled to remind him, "You can call me Graham, you know?"

"Eh, sure, whatever you say, Tettersaw."

I chuckle.

So much for that.

Last names are Jock's shtick. Though I've noticed when shit gets real, he uses first names.

"Okay, so what's this great news, Jock?"

Sliding his reading glasses up the bridge of his nose, he peers down at what looks like a contract of some sort. I've seen enough, I should know.

My heart starts beating like crazy. *Could this be a football deal?* I want this so badly.

As my excitement builds, he says, "I think I have something in the works for you."

I have a shot at making a team? I need to know, but I'm afraid to ask.

But I must.

So, slowly, I murmur, "What kind of something are we talking about here?"

Without looking up from what just has to be a contract, Jock says, "There's a team expressing great interest in you, Graham."

Whoa, he just used my first name. This is the real deal. And that is definitely a contract in his hands.

Fuck.

He goes on, "This team would like to fly you out to their mini-camp. It's going on right now. You could run some reps so they can see you in action, verify your arm is still strong—"

"It is," I interrupt.

Jock talks right over me. "—*and* to make certain your knee is no longer a problem."

I assure him my knee's not an issue at all, and he says, "Good. We'll have to move fast then, if you're interested."

Am I interested?

Is he crazy?

Laughing, I assure him, "I'm interested, Jock. Fuck, trust me, I am."

"Good to hear. If this team likes what they see"—he picks up the contract and waves it in the air, making the screen blur—"they're prepared to follow through on a more-than-fair offer."

My breath catches in my throat. Could this be the shot I've been wishing and hoping for? Hell, the ink's not even dry on my list of new goals.

This is almost too good to be true, though.

So, erring on the side of caution, I inquire, "Which team are we talking about here, Jock?"

He replies "the Columbus Comets," and my heart sinks.

I knew this was too perfect.

"Did you say the Comets?" I verify.

"Yes, the new team in Columbus, Ohio."

I blow out a disappointed breath. "I know who you mean. They're part of the new football league. The one created just last year."

"Yes, that's them," Jock confirms.

"They're not the NFL, Jock."

Instantly, he snaps, "No, Tettersaw, they're not. But we're still talking about a damn fine opportunity."

He's not entirely wrong.

I'm just torn.

Last year, a two-country league emerged. Comprised of twenty-six teams in the US and Canada, this start-up organization managed to cobble together a surprisingly successful inaugural season.

So, yeah, it's not all bad.

"You're right, Jock," I concede, sighing. "But just so you know, the Comets are *not* my first choice by any means."

He chuckles. "I'm sure they're not, Graham. But there's a lot of chatter that this new league is the league of the future. Think about it for a minute. We're talking fan bases in *two* countries. There's so much room for expansion. This is a good opportunity, my man. And the terms the Comets have outlined for you, if you were to be picked up, are more than equitable."

"Ah, hell,"—I run my hand down my face—"I just don't know."

Blowing out a clearly frustrated breath, Jock says, "I'm going to lay it on the line for you. You're not getting any younger, Tettersaw. That means you can pretty much forget about making a comeback in the NFL. The way that league see things, you had your chance. Now you're just a washed-up former star who carries around a history of painkiller problems."

"Hey!" I bristle. "I only had that problem once. And it was ages ago. I've come a long way since then."

Jock is unruffled, no surprise there.

"Hey, hey, don't get pissed at me. I'm just telling you the way it is. You want a chance to start as a quarterback at the professional level?"

"Yes, of course I do," I snap.

"Well, then this is it, my man. To be honest, this could be an opportunity for you to really shine."

"Ha-ha." I chuckle. "You mean like a comet?"

Jock laughs.

He likes that.

"Yes, I guess you could say that," he says.

"Hell, what the fuck do I have to lose?" I say. "Tell the Comets I'm interested, okay?"

"You got it. And for the record, you're making the right decision,

Graham."

"I hope so," I mumble.

He ignores me and goes on. "I'll fax you the contract in a few minutes. You can look it over thoroughly. I'll also book you a flight to Columbus."

"Perfect, thanks."

After we wrap up, I place my cell on the desk. And then I think about what this means.

Following some serious contemplation, I begin to feel pretty good about this opportunity. I mean, hell, everything Jock said to me is true. The Columbus Comets may not be part of the NFL, but they're no chumps. And, more importantly, they're offering me a chance to play professional football again.

So Columbus, Ohio, hmm…

That's a long way from Las Vegas, where I currently live. But this could be the push I've needed to start a life of my own.

I'm not talking football anymore. No. These past few years I've spent so much time helping others that I've kind of neglected my own self. Even my sister tells me that.

And it's true. I have no wife, no girlfriend, no kids, and, outside of the gym business, no real life.

Shit.

Picking up the pen, I add one more goal to my list—*leave Las Vegas and start a new life.*

Yeah, I like that one.

Because, just like in football, in order to win, you have to have forward progress.

Continue reading *Forward Progress* on Amazon:
amzn.to/2s4zM3W